"How are your relationships with men?"

I sat back on the awful couch. *What a strange question.*

"They're fine; I get along better with men than I do with women. Why do you ask?"

She stared me down before she stated, very directly, "I mean intimate relationships."

I felt overwhelmed and my voice cracked when I spoke, "I'm not currently dating anyone…" I was worried and uncertain where she was going with her line of questioning.

The psychologist continued. "If you ever decide to get married, you should seek professional help first." She said it so casually, like it was no big deal.

I felt the need to defend myself. "Why? I get along with men. Just because I am not currently having sex doesn't mean I'm horrible at dating."

She smiled as if I'd said something funny, then handed me a large envelope. "It's all in the report."

I THEE FLED

ARMANDA LAMBERT

CAVERN OF DREAMS PUBLISHING

I THEE FLED

Copyright © 2016 by Armanda Lambert

All rights reserved. No part of this publication may be reproduced, distributed, or transmitted in any form or by any means including photocopying, recording, or other electronic or mechanical methods without the prior written permission of the publisher, except in the case of brief quotations embodied in critical reviews and certain other non-commercial uses permitted by copyright law. For permission requests, contact the author through the website:

www.cavernofdreamspublishing.com

Publisher's Note: This is a work of fiction. Names, characters, places, and incidents are a product of the author's imagination. Locales and public names are sometimes used for atmospheric purposes. Any resemblance to actual people, living or dead, or to businesses, companies, events, institutions, or locales is entirely coincidental.

Ordering Information: Books may be ordered directly through Cavern of Dreams Publishing. Discounts are available for volume orders.

43 Kerr-Shaver Terrace
Brantford, ON N3T 6H8
Phone: 1-519-770-7515

Library and Archives Canada Cataloguing in Publication

Lambert, Armanda, author
    I thee fled / Armanda Lambert ; Bethany Jamieson, Danielle Tanguay, editors ; Kate Pellerin, illustrator.

Issued in print and electronic formats.
ISBN 978-1-927899-35-9 (paperback).--ISBN 978-1-927899-36-6 (pdf)

    I. Title.

PS8623.A482818 2016   C813'.6   C2015-908368-0
                                                                                                C2015-908369-9

FOR BART, WHO REMINDS US THAT HOPE IS ALWAYS WITHIN REACH.

FOR JOHN BUFFALO NATION, A LEADING MAN IN MANY GREAT ADVENTURES.

ACKNOWLEDGEMENTS

I would like to thank the entire team at Cavern of Dreams Publishing for their brilliant contributions and their support. They are just some of the brilliant women who have inspired me in my life.

I would like to thank my parents, for their love and acceptance; my aunt Doris, for always encouraging me to give it a try; and my sisters, for being the kind of women all girls can look up to! Thank you to my brother, Jason, for allowing me the pleasure of learning about the secret world of boys. I love you all.

Prologue

My sisters and I grew up in a townhouse complex during our early youth; it was like the Wild West but with children in charge. It was a time where children minded themselves for most of the day and only ran home when their full names were called for dinner. The complex was located near what was then the outskirts of town, right beside the most popular biker bar. Needless to say, we learned a lot of skills during this time.

Growing up, I never fantasized about getting married like most little girls did; I much preferred playing games pretending to interview people or being a famous movie star. The only times I ever willingly pretended I was married it was always to Michael Jackson—but he was a doctor at the time, not a musician. I just thought medicine was a better-suited career for him, at least if he intended to be my husband.

My sisters loved the romantic notions of marriage, despite being raised by a youthful single mother. Very often, I would be victim to their romantic ideals, having to participate in what I look back on as my first and only marriages. I lovingly refer to them as my *reoccurring bad dreams,* much the same as some look upon their own first marriages.

My wedding day would begin with a good run around the neighbourhood, searching for bugs in the grass and biking around the streets looking for other children to play with. If a wedding was going to happen, I was blissfully unaware. Then, the approach: my sisters, with bored looks in their eyes and wearing salesmen smiles, would come to me with an offer of great fun. Having experienced this before, I would generally say no, but then the negotiations would take place and I would eventually cave; after all, everyone I knew was already at the "venue." I would begrudgingly walk to our backyard to have my hair done; the dandelions were usually already woven into a crown, it having received an invitation to attend prior to me.

My mother's elegant clothes would be pinned and draped lovingly over me until I was so pretty it was simply impossible to walk. My sisters, the self-appointed ringmasters, would run me through a rehearsal of what to say and when to walk, then hand me a bouquet and the ceremony would begin.

With perfect timing the wedding march would start—*"bam-bam-bum-bam"*—and I would try to walk in my mother's heels, carrying the dandelions, while dragging my mother's good dress behind me. Three of our friends would follow until I arrived before the seven-year-old minister. A speech would ensue until someone brought my best friend and me fake rings. He would look at me with what I found to be peculiar pride and say, "I do." Then all eyes were on me, staring with great excitement—except the eyes of my sisters, whose threatening looks clearly warned I was not to deviate from the prescheduled plan; I was not to ruin this event for them. Respectfully I would answer back, "I do." Like all marriages at this point, bated breaths made room for giggles, and the pinted-sized minister would proclaim with devious excitement, "You may now kiss the bride!"

I always clearly heard *may* in the sentence, but you would be shocked how many let it go completely unnoticed. The groom had no apathy toward the word, and I didn't know if he understood it was optional. When I noticed his puckered lips directed at me, as he waited with his warm, inviting eyes, I proclaimed, "I am not kissing him!" Then, like in all good marriages, a family brawl would begin.

Did you know that a marriage is not official unless you kiss? That's right—the entire marriage was reliant on my lips. I learned group peer pressure is a very effective tool, and how happy my best friend became when he got a kiss. It wasn't until fifth year of university that I learned in marriages there is a choice. Looking back, it's fascinating how a group of kids living on assistance, being raised by single mothers and absentee fathers, could possibly want to consider marriage or even hold the ideal as romantic. But my wedding to my best friend was a regular occurrence when boredom hit, and officially the only *I do*'s I have ever said, even under duress.

Throughout my life, I have been around weddings in varied capacity: I have been flower girl, maid of honour, and bridesmaid—some joke I have been everything except the priest and the bride. When I was in my teens, I attended many weddings as a guest, as well as when I was working a part-time job as a videographer. In my early twenties, I attended weddings while running my DJ service, which was around the time everyone I knew was starting to itch for *the ideal*. In my thirties, I attended weddings as a photographer. I can officially say I am not opposed to attending a wedding—when I am being paid.

Over the span of many years, I have seen many who loved one another on the special day abandon the commitment years later, sometimes after only a few months. Too many people get married because they feel it's time, given how long they'd been dating. I have seen marriage to keep a love who threatened to leave if marriage did not take place. Some want to bring a child into the world in the *right* circumstances. The worst marriages are the ones where two people are too afraid of being alone—so anyone will do.

I can see where people may have varied opinions, but I am not opposed to marriage despite saying no to five serious proposals. I can honestly say I have been loved, and loved back to the best of my ability. If I am making a choice as a life commitment, then the reason for marriage *must* matter. Love and choice are relevant, and saying yes must come with the intent to stay committed to the marriage and the vows spoken. If and when I say yes, I will slave away after that love because I hope it gives its soul to me in the same capacity. I will be the great defender of that love because I will consider it a special gift imparted especially to me.

My refusals have never been an issue of commitment as much as a crime of timing. In my adult life, I have had a proposal under duress, a proposal that was a means to an end, a proposal that was the right thing to do under the circumstances, a proposal to please the masses, and a proposal of great passion and anger that was quickly forgotten. I do not grieve over my responses, again because I believe marriage should be a well-thought-out choice.

Despite my early conditioning, I *do* believe in marriage, and that is why I have always said no.

To be or not to be; that is the question….

There have been many moments in my past that lend weight to the theory that I am just not the marrying type, and it should be noted that the top three songs on the day I was born were Paul Simon's "Fifty Ways to Leave Your Lover," Ray Charles' "Hit the Road Jack," and R.B. Greaves' "Take a Letter Maria." One could make a strong argument that my independent nature was predetermined by Top Forty fate, and I think my high-strung behaviour was written into the music of my life. I must come by it honestly; leaving love when it did not feel right has always been easy for me. The music dictated the adventures and heartaches I was meant to live through. The dances I was meant to learn.

I have a very long sheet of inappropriate behaviour toward the opposite sex. When I was four years old, my mother put me in a bath with her friend's son. I remember looking with curiosity at all his parts. I had never seen a boy naked before and I was overwhelmed by his *deformity*. He, being the son of a single mother, thought I made good arguments about him needing corrective surgery. Looking back, it probably was not a good idea for me to offer help, or for the adults to leave us alone that long in a bath. I honestly believed I was helping by using my mother's razor to try to cut it off for him. When he screamed, I reassured him it was going to be okay—our parents felt otherwise. As soon as our mothers entered the room, my mother screamed, "Stop!" and his mother cried at the sight of the blood. She scooped him into her arms and a towel and quickly disappeared while my mother yelled, asking me what I may have been thinking. I repeated I was just trying to help; the conversation that followed led to a new book in the house that explained everyone's parts in a nice, childproof manner. I started to feel bad about what I had done, but I was never able to apologize. They never came back for another playdate.

When I was six years old, I was performing a dance on stage for the church picnic. A boy my age was sitting in the front row, smiling through the first dance. During the second dance, I think he wanted attention, because he started heckling and calling me names. I attempted to calm him with dirty looks, and when that did nothing I looked to the audience for help. It was a powerful moment for me when I realized the only person paying attention to me was this heckling boy. I assumed since no one was paying attention to the performance, no one would notice me leap off the stage to punch the boy in the nose. I was wrong. The very long drive back to our home included a sermon from my mom about how embarrassing my behaviour—in front of the entire congregation—had been for her. That I had no remorse about his bloody nose and tears did not help my case.

Two years after that event I found out the boy's name. My sisters and I attended a French-language school attached to an English-language school, which were separated by a shared gym. During recess, an imaginary line across the middle of the yard separated us, and when we were curious about the *other side,* we would march close to the territory line. One day during this ritual, I heard a bold boy scream across the yard, "Back away, French fry!" I didn't take that well and hollered back "Shut up, English muffin," after which he and his friends decided to start a chant of "French fry," over and over again.

In all fairness, I warned him he should stop because I was getting angry. He boldly replied, "What are you going to do about it, French fry?" I thought it best to show him rather than respond. I ran across the line and pulled him to the ground, where I attempted to give him a bloody nose.

Once the teachers pulled us apart, we were brought to the English principal's office to sit in the same room and wait for our parents. I made no eye contact as I felt very entitled to my actions, and I was still very angry when his parents entered the room with mine. The principal began to explain what had occurred when the boy's mother started to smile. When the principal stopped speaking, his mother took a few steps forward and took a good, long look at me. Then she turned to her son.

"Evan, take a long look at that girl. She is the same girl who gave you a bloody nose at church."

When he turned to look at me I realized she was right, I had given him a bloody nose before.

His mother continued: "My dear son, you know she is the one girl who is almost guaranteed to punch back, so perhaps you should stop picking on her. You know what will happen to you if you don't!"

She then smiled and escorted him out of the room, but not before offering her apologies to my parents.

I never saw Evan at school again but he would later become a lifelong friend. His proposal would also be the most painful to refuse.

When I was seven, I decided to do some *when I grow up* work. I resolved I was going to have five children who all looked like Cabbage Patch Kids; I would look like Claudia Schiffer, but with hair like The Misfits from *Jem and the Holograms*. My wardrobe would be similar to Pat Benatar's, and my husband would be a doctor. In order to break the poker-straight hair curse I bore, my husband would have to have curly hair, and as height was a bit of a challenge for me, it was best he be tall so my children would have that advantage as well. He would be a jack-of-all-trades who could fix anything around the house. His eyes would be green-gold because without the gold he just wouldn't be magic. *Magic is important in love!* He would always have a smile for me, and the children's and his teeth would sparkle like diamonds. I carefully plotted my husband on a scrap piece of paper, put it in an envelope, and sealed it with a kiss.

Yes, at seven years old, the superficial attributes of my husband were imperative, with little to no thought to his demeanour. My husband would just be the best, and all the other women would envy me because he was cuter than their husbands and a great breadwinner. As I got older, this concept did not change all that much.

I have never liked societal expectations of who I should be as a girl or a woman. By eleven years old, I had started my lovely womanly days and begun developing breasts; I say *developing* because until I had children, there was no real evidence growth was occurring at all. I discovered young girls are great educators—I received all sorts of advice! How I should not speak to boys unless my hair was blowing in the wind, how tight clothes make you look better, and that boys like girls who laugh at all their jokes. When walking down the street with a boy, you should be walking with hands in each other's pockets. Most importantly, boys like girls who don't speak, and it is better to lie about your feelings than to be honest about who you are. These ideals were reinforced by the classroom boys' jokes. But the rules were most puzzling to me; they didn't make sense. I felt like an outsider to the culture.

When I was fourteen, Ronald walked me home from school. I was good friends with Ronald, and we would hang out often playing video games, riding our bikes, and listening to music. It was a warm, fall day and as we walked, he turned to me and said, "I think you should be my girlfriend."

Perplexed, I asked, "What does that mean?"

My overtly aggressive tone of disgust should have been a clue to him that I felt violated by his proposal to change our friendship, but he continued.

"It means we would hang out like always, but sometimes I would kiss you and then eventually we would have sex and stuff."

"Are you being funny?" I asked.

"No," he replied.

The idea that he had been thinking of having sex with me did not flatter me; it evoked anger in me. It did not take me long to get him to the ground, but as I lifted my arm to lay down a good punch, he rolled over to avoid the hit. I then sat on his back, and held his head up by his hair with my left hand while my right hand fed him dirt. It was around that time my sisters came walking up and saw what I was doing.

My one sister shouted in shock, "Are you feeding him dirt?!"

When I said yes, we all broke out in laughter. I eventually removed myself, and Ronald stood up. I proudly proclaimed *that* would teach him to ask me out, but he just cleaned himself up as he walked away. He started dating another girl who became pregnant a year later. He would later tell me it was a good thing I never dated him.

The Examination

Although I have never said yes to an engagement proposal, I am remarkably good at calling the probability of a marriage's survival. When you take the time to look at a couple's body language, you can almost see the faultier one show its natural face. Some relationships are like a full glass of wine sitting slightly off the edge of a table, waiting for a perfectly timed brush with an elbow before it falls and reveals the wine all over the floor. It is easier to see the weakness from the outside looking in, or in hindsight. As such, I have always been cynical about the concept and ideals of marriage. When I was at university, I knew many people who found love and became engaged; everyone was in a rush to settle in with a significant other, like somehow it gave them social status or made them more mature than the rest of us. It's been years since those days and I still don't feel like I am mature enough to date, never mind marriage.

I sat on a committee with a man at university who had found the love of his life; she sat on our committee as well. After a meeting, in grand gestures with great smiles and excitement, they made their engagement announcement. Quickly, everyone joined in to congratulate them—except me.

I was too busy dissecting why their marriage was a poor decision to notice the groom-to-be looking at me. He finally said, "Are you not excited for us?"

Suddenly, a familiar look crossed the faces of all present: a look of disgust and worry at what I might say, followed by acknowledgement of my lack of education in social graces and censorship. All eyes begged for a response.

"It's nothing," I said evasively to avoid confrontation.

"No, I want to know what the problem is with us being engaged!" he persisted.

He couldn't let it go so I told him in a proud, unafraid-of-confrontation tone, "It's just that studies show people change the most in their twenties; what's the rush? If it *is* love, why not wait a couple of years? Won't love follow if you make it wait?"

The groom-to-be looked furious as everyone else's faces shifted to a standard, pay-no-attention stance. "What would you do, Sabrina, if the love of your life met you tomorrow? What would you do?"

He had a valid question, and with no further thought or hesitation I replied, "God help him if he meets me tomorrow. I have no time for that; I would probably be mean to him." Strangely, I knew I meant it.

The gasping sounds from the committee suggested my ideals were not generally well received. Maybe I was supposed to be in a rush to find a man, although I could not think of why. My life was in good order: I had a job and a nice apartment. My friends were incredible and fun and I had plenty of hobbies to fill my time. What need did I have for a man? I wasn't ready for kids, so why would I take the little spare time I had to try to achieve social acceptance by finding love? I was happy and content with my life, and yet when others looked in, it was always with pity, like my lack of a relationship was a symptom of some internal problem I had not yet discovered.

During my university years, I learned how to make an *I'm-happy-for-you* face, as it was clear my natural *what-are-you-thinking* face was not appreciated. I also learned how to say "How pretty!"

when I did not mean it, while looking down on a finger graced with a new ring. I even learned to use follow-up questions, like "You must be so excited?" and "Have you set the date?" Those are sentiments appreciated after announcements of the marriage kind.

There are times when I have said these things and meant it; I have been sincerely happy for some who shared, even ecstatic at times. But, I am very good at calling the glass-spill before it happens. I learned at university that it is not always my place to rescue someone from his or her choices. I also concede that, sometimes, I was wrong.

One of my dorm-mates found out she was pregnant in first year; soon after, *the ring* appeared. I was extremely worried it would be detrimental to her life. I tried to explain that she had choices, and a baby didn't mean she had to get married. The *why-not* speech was topped off with a *what-about-your-own-goals-do-you-really-want-to-just-be-his-wife* speech.

My worries were in no way a reflection of how I felt about her fiancé; he was a spectacular guy who treated her as a goddess. He was perfect boyfriend material: goal-oriented, hard-working, and super kind. I was worried their marriage was not a choice made in love but rather in lust or circumstance. She left at the end of that semester, ring on hand, and the two of them are still married to this day, loving each other and their children, making it all look easy and fun.

Toward the end of my first year of university, it was confirmed I might have a different outlook on romantic relationships. I had been struggling in one of my classes so my teacher sent a referral on my behalf to a psychologist to test for a learning disability. They call this test a *psycho-educational examination*. What it meant was I spent two days feeling like a lab monkey. Day one was a *read-this-explain-it, do-you-understand-this-word-what-does-it-make-you-think-of* day; I was shown pictures to label, and then I was sent home with a six-page questionnaire. Questions asking about my ambition, self-viewing, and my fetishes in sexual play. I could not grasp why any of that was relevant to my ability to process information, but I was reassured it was a standard personality test, not to worry, and to answer honestly. I did answer honestly, while trying to decipher what the questions were trying to source.

Day two: I gave the questionnaire back and continued with my role of lab monkey; I had to draw a picture of myself and do some creative writing. When I was finished, I was dismissed, not to return until the results were ready.

By the time they compiled the results, it was summer. I received a formal letter letting me know my allotted time to attend a meeting with the psychologist.

I woke up the day of the appointment unaware of the affirmation the meeting would give me. I had my morning coffee with a bit of anxiety as to what was wrong with my ability to process information; secretly, I was certain I would be diagnosed with a social disorder, as I spent most days feeling as though I had one. That was not at all the case, however.

I walked the two blocks to the office, still apprehensive but excited about finally having answers. I thought it an honour to be given the chance to have a professional review me as an individual and give an opinion about my personality, as well as my potential. I was enthusiastic—until I walked into the office. The heavy wooden door opened with a sound like a dying cat uttering its last plea; the bell at the top of the door officially announced my arrival to the receptionist. Instantly I became aware of my attire: ripped jeans and a sweater. Everyone else was in business-casual clothes. It occurred to me that I *looked* like a lab monkey.

The receptionist asked gently, in a tone that suggested she might be concerned with my stability, if I was the eleven o'clock. I muttered my confirmation then slithered into a wooden chair to await my turn. She smiled gracefully then returned to typing on her computer.

    I am not well known for sitting still, but I was trying to not look crazy, so I did my best not to move. I did not have to wait long before she called me in. The psychologist was composed; she led me in without a word and pointed to a large brown couch beside the door. It was made of hard leather, not conducive to lying down. I wondered how her depressed patients ever relaxed enough to speak. She sat with her back to me going over papers on her desk, which was clear across the room. It was not a warm office.

    She swivelled her chair around to face me and asked, "Do you know why you are here?"

    I replied, "You read the results, do you think I know why I am here?"

    The psychologist didn't laugh so I quickly made my smile into a serious face. She went over my learning disability in detail: what it meant, solutions, and how she came to those conclusions. She advised me the results would be sent to my school. Then, she turned back to her desk and started signing papers. I thought that meant I was dismissed so I started gathering my things.

Hearing me making an exit, she turned and said, "How are your relationships with men?"

I sat back on the awful couch. *What a strange question.*

"They're fine; I get along better with men than I do with women. Why do you ask?"

She stared me down before she stated, very directly, "I mean intimate relationships."

I felt overwhelmed and my voice cracked when I spoke. "I'm not currently dating anyone…" I was worried and uncertain where she was going with her line of questioning.

The psychologist continued. "If you ever decide to get married, you should seek professional help first." She said it so casually, like it was no big deal.

I felt the need to defend myself. "Why? I get along with men. Just because I am not currently having sex doesn't mean I'm horrible at dating."

She smiled as if I'd said something funny, then handed me a large envelope. "It's all in the report."

With that, I was dismissed. I rushed home to read the results but found no explanation. In some ways, I was reassured that she figured out my issues with marriage were a part of my personality; I came by them honestly and wasn't going out of my way to be deviant or offensive. I told my parents about the psychologist's assessment, not in any attempt to kill my mother's dreams, but as a warning it might take me time.

I knew my issues with marriage were ingrained in my psyche long before I ever received a marriage proposal; my suitors would be clearly warned I had a risk of offending. Some of the problem lay with the men in my life and their perception that I was some great obstacle to overcome. My personality was seen as stubbornness, or it was assumed I was acting out from a prior bad relationship. It seemed the more I said no to men, the more frequent and extravagant their gifts became. All thought a knee on the floor would override my innate nature, and although I had been honest, I still chose to partake.

Armanda Lambert

The Pee-wee Herman Summer

Home from university, I was watching a late night show. The guest was Paul Reubens, otherwise known as Pee-wee Herman. He had already been through success and jail and was out and about, chatting about his time spent doing both. When the host asked what he was doing currently, he answered that he was now accepting any and all proposals. He went on to say he had been to a few great parties with fans and just wanted to enjoy what life would bring his way.

    I thought this was brilliant. I had dated a few people while away at university but nothing to write home about. I thought, *rather than me picking who I would date, knowing how good my taste had been, maybe I would just let* them *pick* me*.* I could make a few rules, be forthcoming, and say yes to each and every offer for a summer. I would pay no mind to the approach, as I often got caught up on that. I would intentionally overlook their physique or any facial attributes. Careers and goals would simply not matter to me. Maybe I could find a good man by accident or default. At worst, I would have an interesting summer.

My only rules were: I will not sleep with you, and I am in no way exclusive. I surmised that we were all adults, and if those two things were going to be a problem then the suitor's participation was not necessary.

Off I went, waiting for fate to throw me a prince.

My first invitation came from a good friend of mine's ex-husband. Although that sounds strange, the two of them were older than me and very amicable. I never understood why she left him; then again, I was never made privy to the details. He was a fair-looking man with a little bit of red in his hair, intensely smart and charming, and we had hung out together many times before. He worked in theatre and invited me to attend a cast party after the opening of a show.

I did not explain the rules to him, as I was not concerned with his interest in me. I always enjoyed my time with him; he spoke in such a way I would inevitably learn something about life and my place within it through his insight.

The party was loud, with a big dance floor right in the middle of the room. I felt a little out of place as he was the evening's DJ and I knew only a few people in attendance. I watched all night as people approached to make requests for songs and together we would laugh about the choices; we were both music snobs. There was one woman who repeatedly came up to the table. She was gorgeous, with a tall, slender build and long, blond hair. Her face was flawless with her painted red lips. When she and my friend spoke, she appeared to be as charming as he was, and it was obvious she was deeply amused by him when her perfect hands landed on his shoulder to whisper closely in his ear. She was not new to the game and she knew what she wanted.

I thought that would be a good time to disappear for a while and give him space; he didn't need to have eyes on him. I went to the bar to get us refills.

When I got back I gave him an eye and asked, "Well, did you get her number?"

He quickly replied, "No, why would I do that?"

I smiled and bantered back, "Are you kidding me? She is stunning and obviously into you."

His reply was life-changing for me and I will never forget it. With a great seriousness, he said to me, "Why would I take her home? I don't need to find love, I already found the one I love. Circumstance does not change that for me." I knew he meant it. He had a great loyalty to his love, my friend, his ex-wife, even while respecting the boundaries she had laid out for him. Truth be told, when things went wrong it was him she relied on. He would stay away when she wanted, and just take the parts she was willing to give because he truly loved her. On the way out that night, a man stopped me. He was wearing a nice suit, had light hair and soft features, and he handed me a business card as he asked if I wanted to go out sometime. Had it not been my Pee-wee Herman Summer, I would have found this approach very tacky, maybe a little too bold. However, it was *that* summer, and I had made a commitment to myself. I promptly said yes, following the rules. He said the rules were fine and we agreed to meet the next day, as he was in town but did not reside in the area.

Brian picked me up around seven the next night in his very tidy new car. He was wearing a more casual outfit, but still presentable enough to attend a family gathering. During our drive to the bar, it occurred to me he looked familiar, like we had met before. He spoke about how his parents lived in town and he was down visiting, but that he owned a home in a town about an hour away. He was thirteen years older than I was, which, at that moment, I didn't care about, and he was a French math teacher. He did not come from a French background but he knew it would be easier to get employment if he was able to teach in French. I thought that was a sign of intelligence on his part, and I listened and marvelled that I could learn so much in such a short car ride.

Brian seemed to have his whole life in order: good family, good job, a house. The most interesting things I had to offer were a few jokes and a nightly ritual of being a mascot for the local ball team. Surprisingly, that was very amusing to him as he also coached the girls' basketball team at the high school where he was employed.

We pulled up to a cocktail bar that I had never gone to before, mostly because I knew how expensive it was. I was looking forward to seeing how it looked inside, and secretly I felt as though that was how adults dated: fancy dresses, suits, and overpriced vodka. Brian graciously asked me where I preferred to sit, at a table or at the bar, and I chose the bar. We sat side by side and ordered our drinks as I looked around to see what the bar had to offer aside from drinks and dull lighting.

There was mellow music playing but not from a live band, and there were no dartboards or pool tables. When I turned back and looked at Brian, I still could not shake the feeling that we had met before.

"Do I look familiar to you? 'Cause I think we may have met before," I said. Turned out, I was right; one martini later we figured out he had been my substitute teacher two years prior.

When he asked what I wanted to do next, leaving the mellow bar was at the top of my list. We found a place that had good beer on tap, a live band, and a pool table. This is a good time to mention I can play a fair game of pool. After beating Brian three times, he offered to take me home. He was very much a gentleman and opened my door when he dropped me off. He went to walk me to my door, but I explained how that was not necessary and he respectfully let it be. We made plans to get together another day and said farewell.

The next yes I said was to a man I had known for a few years. I knew he was a womanizer but I had forewarned him of the rules. He had a slick smile and stunning brown eyes, and his physique gave women the impression he could haul them over his shoulder and run a marathon. He was a car salesman and nine years older than me. I had always had a secret crush on him, and given our history, I felt very comfortable with him.

Carl and I had a blast over dinner, laughing about times past. Our familiarity made dinner conversation easy to come by, and as he spoke, I could see he was more vulnerable than I had ever perceived. He was like a little boy trapped in a hot man's body, insecure but all the while intensely confident in how women perceived him. After dinner, we shared laughs while we walked back to the car; then, he did this *thing*—a thing I felt was unbecoming and disrespectful of him.

Carl opened my door but then blocked the entrance with his body so I couldn't get in. I didn't know what to make of it, and thought maybe he was just caught up in his story.

"Let's get going," he said, but still didn't move out of the way. He had said *let's get going* like it was an invitation, so I walked toward him thinking he would move. Instead, he leaned in and landed a kiss on me before I knew what was going on.

When he had first leaned in to kiss me, I was angry about how it happened, but as I lay in bed that night I was grateful he had kissed me. It had reminded me there was something to be said for chemistry; I had been kissed by a man I had always wanted to kiss, whom most women found attractive, and yet I felt nothing. There was nothing wrong with his style of kissing or technique, and I had had a great time over dinner, yet when he dropped me off, I think we both knew it was not going to work. We did not make any special plans to hang out again, and that was the last time we saw each other. Sadly, he passed away a month later in his sleep.

I started to date Mark, the lead pitcher of the ball team I was working for. It happened very casually; there was no real invitation. After every ball game, the staff and players would go to dinner at the restaurant that sponsored the team. Mark was an exceptional pitcher, and there's not much to say about him except he was kind and gorgeous, with blond hair and a perfect pitcher's build. Sitting with him left all the other girls with perfect green eyes full of envy. I did not take pleasure in their jealousy, but I did feel like I was saving him, somehow, from the treacheries of gold-digging fingers that the gutter birthed—those trying to grab him before fame. Everyone knows this type of girl; she is easy to spot in a crowd: half-dressed, with the *willing-to-be-a-baby-mama* look in her eyes, while she carries her daddy issues in her purse. She pretends to like the game so she can get to the player's house for a little one-on-one. I was not one of those girls and I took pride in it, and Mark was so kind and far too good for them! He was the best pitcher the team had that summer; however, he had no personal aspirations of playing pro ball. Instead, he had talent and a family legacy to honour, and he would often talk about not letting his dad down. Mark just wanted to write children's books.

Mark and I would hang out casually from time to time and only kissed one night. It was an awkward experience because he shared a basement with three other players from the team. He was very sweet, and I rollerbladed home with a warm feeling about the night.

Nothing ever came of it as fate has a way of leading you where it wants you to go. The following night at the game, he waved to me from the pitcher's mound and threw his arm out with the next ball he pitched. He left for home that same week. The fans are a superstitious sort and I came to believe some of them thought it was my fault he got hurt. I would rather think the gods knew he had a great story to write and the ball game was getting in his way.

Shortly after Mark went home, I attended a wedding with Brian. Being as he was thirteen years older than I was, all his friends were starting to get married. I wasn't overly excited about going; in fact, I spent the morning of the wedding working on a painting of Eve and the snake, minus the apple.

When I started to get ready for the evening, I had to use brake fluid to wash the black paint off my hands because I was desperate to remove it and nothing else was working. As I dressed, it occurred to me how much work this Pee-wee Herman idea had turned out to be. I felt like every night I was putting on a new dress for events that I did not consciously decide to attend. But I was still committed and optimistic about the idea.

Brian picked me up as usual and complimented me on my attire; he looked very handsome as well. Not once during the long car ride did he mention the faint smell of brake fluid, which I thought was rather nice of him. It was a long drive to Toronto from my house, and we mostly listened to the radio and discussed our musical tastes. Brian always seemed to be pleased with my talk of work as well. Although my jobs were nothing like his career, I never felt it was an issue.

The wedding ceremony was elegant. During the day a traditional Catholic Church wedding, and then an early evening Japanese ceremony by candlelight. The bride wore a hot pink traditional dress and her husband a suit. Her family looked on with tremendous pride, so much so that when her grandmother cried I almost joined in.

When we sat at our table at the reception, I was introduced to three other couples. It is always strange to meet the friends of someone you are dating, especially when it has only been a couple of dates and the introductions take place at a wedding. All of them had attended high school with Brian, and they all knew everything about one another. When one of his friends asked me where I worked, although I was holding down more than one job, I panicked and blurted out, "I am a mascot for the single A division ball team."

The looks and *right-ons* from the men signalled great approval; their wives, however, were not going out of their way to make me feel I would ever be invited into their homes. They had done their time birthing babies, made the commitments, and were not going to have some girl, half their age and half their size, charm their husbands. Their feelings were clear, not just in the condescending language they used but in their faces every time they looked at my date. In all fairness, I did not look my age and Brian's friends high-fiving him was not helping. On the way home, during that very long drive, I brought it up. I thought I was gentle about it.

"So did you notice all the wives hated me?" I said, smiling.

You know that moment when someone is gathering themselves and preparing to lie to save face? That was the moment Brian was having before he looked at me in the most convincing way and said, "Just give them time to get used to the idea."

It had been a long day and I am naturally temperamental, so this may have been our first spat, so to speak.

"Do you mean give them time to get used to being polite?" I called a spade a spade: their protest of our dating was loudly received with every one of their childish tactics.

Brian, for the first time, was not amused with my response. "You *are* a lot younger than me!"

I thought it best to clarify. "You mean I'm only two years older than your students?"

I don't think the age difference bothered me until the very moment I said it. I was two years older, but I still looked younger than his students. Brian and I didn't talk much after that; we didn't even make plans for another visit when he dropped me off at home. He drove away without saying goodbye. I assumed he was done with me.

A couple weeks and a few more dates went by before I saw Brian again, and I must admit I was a little shocked. It was my birthday and I was working at the ballpark. I looked up in the stands, and there was Brian looking back at me with a smile. I was not very excited to see him because I was working and knew he would want some attention. But, as I have mentioned, Brian was a very tactful man and did not approach me until after the game.

With a big card in his hand he said, "Hope you didn't think I forgot your birthday; let me take you out."

I had no other plans at that point and he looked so endearing so I thought, *why not?* He had planned that we would go mini putting, something I am terrible at.

I asked, "Why mini putting? Why not a pool hall?"

What he replied and what would follow that day would be my justification for ending the Pee-wee Herman phase. With a very sincere and honest look he said, "Well, when we play pool you always win, and you mentioned you're not good at mini putting, and well, I am."

I was confused and thought maybe I didn't hear him correctly; after all it was *my* birthday, not his. "So we are only doing this so you can beat me at something? Is that right?"

We had arrived so he didn't respond, he just got out of the car and opened my door for me. In my mind, I was wondering why my beating him was an issue, and how had I not noticed until he told me?

"You ready?" Brian asked.

The weather was warm with no wind, and I knew that would not help my game. Brian walked me to the tiny pencils and helped me pick out a club; it was very charming. He playfully told me how I was going to lose and mocked my shots and we both laughed. It ended up being so enjoyable, I almost forgot the conversation we'd had; I was having too much fun with him and enjoying a view of the *real* him. Finally, the side that was unpolished and playful! A side that held no concern for the vote of others. Although short-lived, I felt privileged to see it. I was quickly brought back to reality after we putted our last hole. Brian eagerly started tallying up the score to see who won, although I did not feel it was necessary as I was very aware of my aptitude in the event. He insisted though, and you could tell it meant a lot to him. I watched his eyes focus as his hands moved the tiny pencil around the sheet. He counted twice.

"You won, by two strokes," Brian said resentfully.

I had no idea what to say. I had never seen a grown man become that upset over a game before. I am not very good with other people's emotions, but I'm especially not good with emotions that seem out of place to me. Brian was visibly upset, like he owed a bookie more than he owned. I said the only thing that could possibly be right to say, or so I thought.

"Are you positive? It must be a mistake. Maybe you just counted it wrong."

For the record, I spoke softly with the intent of being comforting. Brian's response, however, would in no way let you think that. It is best described as an angry and disgusted bad actor trying to play the part of Shirley Temple. This look, mixed with a stomping walk toward the exit, made me wonder if I should even follow, but I did because by then I was offended.

"Are you okay?" I asked as we approached the car, despite already knowing the answer. To his credit, Brian did stop and turn to face me before replying.

"Am I okay...with what, you beating me? Wait, maybe you didn't beat me because I am a math teacher and maybe I counted wrong!"

He paused to open my door, and I stood in shock trying to strategize my exit.

"I wasn't trying to be offensive, everyone makes mistakes," I stated as I got in the car.

Brian got in his side, started the engine, and in a much calmer voice muttered, "It's not enough that you won."

I have to admit I resented the implication and was no longer amused, enamoured, or respectful of his current plight.

"Well, maybe we could try playing another game, not pool, not mini putting," I stated. With hate in my voice I continued, "Any other game—then I can beat you at that too!"

We didn't talk much after that. When we pulled onto my street I couldn't wait to get out of that car; my neck was strained from trying to keep my eyes looking out the window, as far from him as possible. You can imagine my frustration when he drove past my house and parked at the end of the road instead.

"Why are we parked here, did you forget where I live?" I fumed.

"No," he said before he nervously continued, "I have been thinking about life and what I want for my future." As he paused to catch his breath, I could not believe this was what he wanted to share with me after the day we'd had. "I want children and a house with a dog in the yard and I want to do these things with you."

I felt all my nerves snap out of shock with his words and go straight into alert, as if I were on some sort of drug.

"I don't know how to tell you this, Brian, but that's not me—*it's not me!* I don't want a house with kids and a dog and a husband; it's never been my dream. I am too young to even consider."

I was angry as he pulled out his grandmother's wedding ring and continued stretching his arms out to present it.

"Sabrina, when you know who you love, you tell them. Say yes, marry me."

He looked desperate and sad and I was so angry to be in this position after only a couple of dates—we had never even kissed. If this was what I got for being open to new adventures, I was officially done with it.

"No. No!" I don't think it was kind that I said it twice, but in my defence it just sort of happened. "No I will not marry you; I have to go."

I had unlocked the car door with no intention of ever looking back when he softly said, "Can I at least have a kiss goodbye?"

I should have uttered another no, but instead I leaned in, kissed him, and cruelly said, "As long as goodbye is the operative word." I slammed the door.

Walking home seemed like the better option than having him drive me; I was so angry at his audacity to use marriage as a ploy to keep things together after a tantrum. He was obviously unaware or simply did not care about me, or he would have known it was the wrong card to play. We were at different stages in our lives with drastically different ambitions. I also knew I wasn't dealing with having to be the loser for a moment longer. That was the finale of my Pee-wee Herman summer. It would not be repeated.

Still, it felt strange saying no to him—after all, he was a very good-looking man with a solid income. Yet I could not see, nor appreciate, how good looking he was because his personality got in the way.

My mother had a much harder time getting over my refusal of Brian; she had always hoped I would settle down, and marriage seemed to be the right way for me to do so from her point of view. She was very opposed to the lack of loyalty my summer had offered. She especially did not like how it looked to the neighbours when so many different men were picking me up so frequently. It's good for me that I never much cared what people thought of me; my personal life was always just my personal business, not to be justified to anyone but me. I am the one that has to live with the consequence.

The relationship and marriage proposal that followed that summer taught me about the consequences of trying to be what others expect. Where Brian taught me the right formula does not equal the right relationship, Fred would teach me that a game face falls apart behind closed doors.

I Thee Fled

Green Eyes and Silent Tongues

I can clearly remember the night I met Fred. I had just worked a long shift at the dirtiest bar in town. I was desperate for fast cash when I took the job, so when I say dirty, I mean the lights were kept low so you couldn't see the filth lurking in the corners. The dance floor was always full of aspiring strippers who had neither the looks nor the body to ever make it to a club, and the crowd was full of pimps hoping to make a name for themselves on the dancers' self-esteem. It was not a place ever mistaken for a classy bar; it's where you went for a career hooker to take you to the parking lot; the place where if you knew the password, the bartender could serve you up your drug of choice.

    I learned so much watching that community of people slither after dark, and yet, that was where I met Fred. I had just finished locking up the bar and taking the three stone steps down to the sidewalk and there he was, standing in the rain, leaning against his car. No umbrella, just the moonlight, rain, him, and me.

"Can I help you?" I asked with suspicion. No girl likes to find herself unprotected in the dark with a stranger, and I was not taking another step forward until he explained himself.

"I noticed you in the bar and I was thinking we should go out for coffee sometime," he said, rather boldly I thought, but I liked the confidence it showed.

"Who are you?" I asked a little softer than my first greeting.

"Fred. Can I have your phone number?"

At first I laughed. Then I went ahead and introduced myself while I wrote down my number using the pen and paper he already had on hand. I let him drive away before I continued my walk home. I remember thinking, *he's not even that cute, why did I give him my number? Should have given him a fake one. Maybe I'll just avoid him...* All of those things seemed like a good plan, and looking back, any one of those plans would have been the smarter thing to do than the choices that would follow.

Two days after we met, like clockwork, the phone rang. It was Fred, trying to confirm coffee. Coffee always seems so harmless; a short commitment of time, where easy, small talk can be made. Coffee shops usually have many exits and you could possibly run into someone you know, which gives you an out if you need one. Even if you end up not seeing anyone, coffee never promises to take too much time—you can always get out just by drinking faster. I told Fred he could pick me up at seven.

It should have been a warning sign when Fred began talking about his ex-fiancée on our first date, but I just took it as an opportunity to explain my views on marriage. He seemed disheartened and tried to convince me that marriage was a good thing; he wanted it for himself. I explained that we might not be well-suited, but he explained I was under no pressure; he was willing to wait.

There were parts of Fred I found pathetic, such as his taste in music, books, and art. He had a bit of an ego issue, but also a good sense of humour, and he seemed to be responsible and generally nice. Overall, he was fun.

On our fourth date we kissed goodnight, and it was that fourth-date-kiss that made me forget his annoying traits. I don't know if it was just the lack of physical attention I'd experienced for so long that made his kiss like an addiction, but when I went to bed that night all I kept thinking was *he may not be that cute or that smart but he can kiss like a pro.*

After our fourth date we began spending all of our time together, and everything was going well. He was supportive of my writing and photography, and even let me control the car radio. This said a great deal, because if there was anything Fred loved it was his sports car; it was the height of his pride and he loved it over all else. He had saved his money and bought it flat out, polished and washed it once a week, and cared for all its repairs. It was not long at all before he was pushing me to move in with him.

Moving day had very little stress as I was just moving from my parents' basement to his parents' basement. Fred's dad was rarely home but his mother, Linda, was there every day. I liked Linda. She was a recovering alcoholic and all Fred's good traits came from her. The basement was set up as its own apartment with a separate door so we had plenty of privacy, but I made a point of visiting with Linda every day.

It was shortly after moving in with them when Fred began to change. We still went to the bars sometimes, but we started going out less and less, mostly keeping our extracurricular activities to activities of the bedroom. That became such a frequent occurrence I started to pity his parents being upstairs from us. He started with little things, like asking why I was putting on makeup—only whores wore makeup—and telling me that my pants weren't proper for a girl. I started to feel trapped and depressed, but his skills in the bedroom made me forget or start rationalizing that his behaviour might be worth putting up with. It was not rational; it was the start of the decline. The decline, however, was only from my perspective.

It was a warm summer day and I had just come in from a walk. I went to visit with Linda and have some iced tea. Everything seemed ordinary, except my birthday was fast approaching.

"I think Fred is thinking about proposing to you for your birthday," Linda said calmly, like it was not such a big deal.

Painfully aware I was speaking to his mom, I replied, "I hope not because I would say no. He knows how I feel about marriage. I don't think he would do that." But I could tell by her strangely evasive eyes that she already knew Fred was not necessarily thinking, but rather planning.

It is a terrible thing to impose on someone's birthday, especially with a ring. The next two days went by without any more talk of a proposal, and I secretly wished such an embarrassing scene would not take place. Fred and I had only been dating for a short two months; marriage was the last thing on my mind. I wanted more time to think about the relationship, given his newfound jealousy over everyone I talked to, especially men. Did I want to live my life explaining the long traditions of makeup and women, or of how girls dream of being old enough to wear fancy shoes? Were those things I would be willing to live without, just to be someone's wife? If I were truly in love with him, would all these things be minute and irrelevant?

My birthday came before I had the chance to reflect on all my questions. This birthday would go down in my record books as the most imposing proposal of my life.

The morning was normal; Fred and I talked about having dinner to celebrate after work and that was fine with me. I carried on about my day more slowly than usual, trying to avoid what felt like the inevitable. I ate my lunch trying to reassure myself he would know better than to ask. Fred's behaviour had not been out of the ordinary in any way; no sneaky trips to a jewellery store, so, probably, it was going to be okay.

I arrived home at the same time as always. There were cars lined up and down the driveway. When I walked into the house, it was full with his family waiting to greet me: sisters, nieces, and nephews—even his in-laws. I wanted to be grateful for their kindness in throwing me a birthday party, but I looked around and did not see any of my own family. I was still standing at the doorway when Fred hollered, "Hurry up, come sit down!" I knew by sitting I was playing my role in the great production he was conducting; this party was not for me at all.

After I sat, Fred quickly got down on one knee, and instinctively I started shaking my head no, whispering as discreetly as possible to him, "Please don't do this."

He didn't let that stop him, though; instead he began, "Since the first date we had, I have known that I want to spend the rest of my life with you." I know it's customary to look at someone when they are speaking to you, but I was only looking at him because I was afraid of seeing the hope in his family's eyes. "I went the next day and had a jeweller make a ring I designed for you." I could not believe what I was hearing; he had a ring made the day after I told him I never wanted to get married? It was insane!

Then he uttered the words: "Sabrina. Will you marry me?"

Just like that—wedding proposal number two. I looked up at his family and their smiles, except his mother, who wore a look of curiosity. The moment was reminiscent of how it felt when I was young and played wedding with all the kids—having his family witness took away the choice; if I said no, I wasn't just hurting the proposer, but the dreams of the young nieces and nephews watching. I felt trapped. Fred waited with bated breath and a big smile on his face. It was not what I wanted, and I had been very clear about that. I was not going to lie for the sake of his family.

"I am not ready for marriage," I said clearly, and everyone instantly became awkward and tried to look away, "but I'm not planning on leaving you, so if you want me to wear the ring, I will."

Everyone immediately perked up as Fred slid the ring on my hand, and they started celebrating, as if something good had actually happened. I was so distraught I could not even fake a smile. I went to my parents' house and they came back to the party with me and ate corn at the picnic table. I wanted to cry, to tell them everything, but there were too many spectators and I couldn't sneak off with them alone under Fred's ever-growing green eyes. He had heard what I'd said, and although he was smiling, we both knew I viewed that ring as the equivalent of the iceberg to the *Titanic*.

On a night shortly thereafter, a friend of Fred's invited us out to watch him play in a band. I was excited because we hadn't been out in a long time. We both got dressed up with enthusiasm, and I thought it was going to be a good night. Fred bought the first round at the bar while I secured the pool table for us;

we laughed and played all night while I sipped my rum and coke, and he his beer.

It wasn't until we got home that I discovered it had not been a good night at all; Fred's laughter and smile had given me the wrong impression. I had taken off my coat and shoes and started walking toward the bedroom when I heard Fred from down the hall: "Where do you think you're going?"

Startled, I answered "To bed." There may have been a hint of sarcasm in my tone.

"Not in *the* bed," he responded with a glare.

I readily admit I am a little socially stupid, but in spite of my drinking, I was positive it wasn't a moment I should understand. Lucky for me, Fred put his face right close to mine so I would understand clearly.

"My mother is a fucking alcoholic and you smell like her drink of choice. Sleep on the fucking couch! How could you fucking do this to me?"

I was instantly angry and realized he probably shouldn't drink; it was unbecoming of him.

"Why would you keep bringing me your mother's drink of choice all night if you knew it would make you feel this way? How would I know what she drank? How could you? You sleep on the fucking couch!" It was the nicest thing I could respond with, given the level of hate with which he had spoken to me. Fred muttered,

"Fuck you," but he slept on the couch. I locked the bedroom door that night and started thinking I should take a serious look at how my life was looking.

In the morning, the *sorry* and *I love you* washed the air from the night before, the kisses bribed me into another try and for a short time, it wasn't bad. The façade of normality was back and my melancholy seemed unjustified. Fred and I spent more time with his family, who were all very kind and fun, and I hardly noticed how little time I was spending with my friends and family anymore. Although I still wrote, I did so in secret, and my camera mostly stayed locked away under the bed.

Before long the winter was settling in and I was getting excited for my work's Christmas party; I had bought a new suit and shoes to match. It had been so long since Fred and I had been out, I couldn't wait. Fred seemed much less excited, however. He started his propaganda about a week before the event, about how it wouldn't be fun and it would be a stupid night, both of which were ridiculous arguments.

Late afternoon the day of the Christmas party, I had started to get ready before Fred came home from work when his mother called me and asked that I go see her. When I got to her room, she handed me a gift.

"It's nothing big," she said, "I just thought of you when I saw it."

I opened it up to find two writing notebooks and a pen. I smiled. "Thank you, I love it," I said as I gave her a hug.

"Has anyone told you I am a recovering alcoholic?" Linda asked. After I shamefully answered yes, she smiled and continued, "I bet no one told you how I got that way. It started when I first got married; I was an outgoing girl and social, but Ken was not. I was always in the house waiting for him, and soon I started drinking before he got home so I could cope with him. Then I started drinking when he left the house so I could soothe myself from him. My generation does not get divorced."

As I held my books, I realized Linda could hear much more upstairs than she had previously let on, and although she did not say why she was suddenly sharing, I knew already.

"I did not choose to be an alcoholic; I just sort of picked it up when I was losing myself. Fred doesn't want to go to your work party, but I think that's his problem to deal with, not yours." With that, Linda grinned and wished me a good night. As I excused myself and went to go to the stairs, she whispered, "Don't give in, honey."

When Fred arrived home he told me his stomach hurt, and if I loved him, I would stay home and nurse him, but his mother's words sat heavily on my mind. I took a cab out for the night, leaving him at home.

The party was lovely and everyone I liked was there. Many wondered why I was alone but the illness explanation seemed to satisfy their curiosity. I had only been there an hour and a half, just enough time to finish my dinner, when I was paged to the bar for a phone call. No surprise, it was Fred.

"I'm at the hospital. I need you to come get me," he whined.

Annoyed, I asked, "Why are you at the hospital?"

"That's how sick I am and you left me alone!"

It sounded so manipulative that I stayed for two more drinks before I called a cab. I found him sleeping in the emergency ward and it angered me to see how healthy he looked. He opened his eyes, not when I arrived, but rather when the doctor came in.

"What's wrong with him?" I asked.

The doctor's answer was another one of the signs, declaring that it was against my better judgment not to run clear away from the madness.

"Nothing. Has he been under severe stress?" the doctor asked.

"No," I said sternly for Fred's benefit.

"Well, he stressed himself so much that he caused his muscles to go into spasm. We gave him some muscle relaxants, so he should be fine. But he might want to talk to his family doctor about managing stress and anger."

I quickly responded, "You mean he did this to himself?"

The doctor looked perplexed and concerned. "Well, yes. You can sign him out at the desk."

Lucky me, I thought. Fred and I did not talk on the way home. I drove his car without a driver's permit, all the while thinking how he had done this to punish me for attending my own work party. I was angered it only took him an hour and a half to put himself into this state, the state his mother warned me about. It was crazy.

The same crazy led Fred to beg for forgiveness in the morning with passionate kisses that left me void of courage to go. Mixed with the threats of taking his own life, it was enough to hold me in the basement sleeping beside him at night. I fell asleep most nights weighing the pros and cons of our relationship, and reaching for my survival instincts to get through the day. I understood Fred's mother's illness more and more, and I admired her every breath; I could barely breathe with him on me more and more, as if he knew I was strategizing an exit plan.

A month later we moved into an apartment across town. I had thought things were bad before we moved! I soon realized the past had been a warning covered in cotton candy, and the beast in both of us would be exposed.

The beast in me had become unsettled and the one in him never slept. Having no one else living with us meant there were no longer witnesses to our life. The front door closed and the tantrums were easily hidden from the rest of the world. The morning would rise and I would put a game face on until I returned home to shut the door again, increasingly feeling trapped and depressed. I started to wonder if Fred even liked me, despite how often he would tell me he loved me, so much so he would kill himself if I ever left. I was young enough to believe that might be true. I tried to do better and make it work.

I don't think you ever truly know what you would do in a moment of hate until you find yourself doing it. After only a couple of months of living together, I found myself having hateful thoughts. When Fred was late coming home from work, I would hope it meant he had gotten in a car accident and would never come home. I would quickly scold myself for thinking that way until he came home and the stress started again. It was the little things, like interrupting me if I was on the phone until it was pointless to continue a conversation at all, or insisting on a full report of what I did at work, or every detail of the conversations I had. If I missed a detail, he would inform me because he had now taken to driving by and spying on me at lunchtime. Needless to say, Fred always found something I had done during my lunch hour that was unbecoming of a woman. The difference was there were no longer sweet kisses that followed his accusations, just hateful door slams and threats of his impending death if I continued to be myself. I would whisper while I talked on the phone, for his comfort, hoping not to set him off, but it was never enough. I learned I could never comfort the beast in him.

    One day, I spent the day with Fred's niece while his sister was at work. His niece was an adorable little girl who very much liked being girly and fancy. In preparation for our day together, I had gone and purchased two brightly coloured plastic wine glasses for us to drink our apple juice from. We spent a great day doing our nails and makeup, and had a fancily set table to eat our Kraft Dinner. It had been a very long time since I'd had a good day, and I was completely indulgent with her and all the joy she was bringing to it.

Her mother came and picked her up around 4:30 and I began cleaning the house. We had made such a mess that I left the wine glasses in the kitchen sink to tend to later while I took a break from the cleaning. Fred came home and again asked how the day transpired; I told him all about the fun his niece and I had eating a fancy lunch, then continued cleaning without a thought to what I could have done wrong that day. Looking back, I shouldn't have been shocked he could find something. "What the fuck?" was the scream that gave it away, but I had nothing left; I hated him so much I didn't care. *What could it possibly be this time? Does it matter?*

Fred came violently around the corner, clenching the two plastic glasses like they were to be the weapons of my destruction.

"Are you fucking cheating on me?" he asked in such a way I knew he wanted me to take him seriously, and he said it with such force the neighbouring apartments must have known how serious he was as well. He asked with such dramatic intensity, but I truly had nothing left.

With hands clenched into fists and spit on my face, I laughed. One would say right in his face, except that was not my intent, just his poor choice of placement during questioning. Seething with rage, I quietly replied, "Yup, I snuck a hunk of a man into our bedroom and I fucked him all afternoon while your niece sat on the couch and listened. Then, because I am that classy of a whore, I served him wine in plastic fucking glasses that smell like apple juice, you stupid fucking asshole!"

I am not proud of this or the following moments, but like I said I had nothing left, and maybe if he heard what he had been begging to hear, the beast in him would just go on its way.

Fred stood in shock and hoped I didn't notice him sniffing the cups, but there was no hope—it was not going to be a depressing death; it was now a joyous burial dance. I was long overdue for a good argument.

"When I wore makeup to work it's because I was fucking some guy at lunch; you know because you watch from the car and probably jerk off"—I did not even take a breath, afraid he might interrupt—"and my friends that are girls? Well they're not just girls, they're fucking dykes so I fuck them too! I fuck the trees, the car, and anything else I might see! You have been right all this time—well done, Fred! Good for you, Fred! I am fucking leaving, FRED!"

It should have been clear by my rant that I no longer cared, but Fred was not of sane mind. He dropped the glasses on the floor and ran to the bathroom like a child who was outrunning a spider and slammed the door. I thought, *that was easy*, and had made my way to the bedroom to pack my clothes when he started to scream from the bathroom.

"I'm going to kill myself if you go, I mean it!"

I no longer believed he ever meant it, but I was taking the bet, just in case.

"Go ahead," I said.

"I will," he replied.

Back and forth, we went on like toddlers. When my bag was packed, Fred was still hollering from the bathroom. As I walked past, I opened the door. He was just standing there, staring with a red face into the mirror. All I saw was a manipulative, pathetic liar. I ran to the kitchen as he stared, now unsure of his power, and grabbed him a knife—a big, old, horror-film-style butcher knife—brought it to the bathroom and placed it on the counter.

"I would think you'd need this at a moment like this, wouldn't you?" I said as I stared him down; I wanted to see the look in his eyes when I called his bluff. I then took two steps back, never leaving his stare, and dialled his mother's number. Linda answered, unsuspecting of the moment.

"Hello?"

How sweet her voice was. My head began to clear.

"Your son is in the bathroom threatening to kill himself and I must leave."

I said it because it was true; I had to leave. I had so much hate for Fred, he was now safer in a bathroom threatening to kill himself than he was if he were left with me in an apartment full of various weapons. I dropped the phone without a plan, grabbed my bag, and went to the closest payphone to beg my mother to come quickly in case he followed me out.

It took Fred many months to accept it was over, even more for him to take the ring back. I would later admire my ring on another woman's hand when she was sharing her news with a stranger in a bar bathroom; I guess he could live without me—if I had only believed that earlier.

Linda would later tell me she was proud of me and glad I got out. She would call from time to time to let me know when the boys would be out so I could sneak over for a visit. It happened less and less as life moved on, but I will always be grateful for her talks and wisdom. I learned things about myself through her eyes, and even more about the hidden strength that can appear when you least expect it. I decided if I had listened to my instincts in the first place, the whole

Fred stage could have been avoided, and perhaps, moving forward, I would take that into consideration.

I left Fred, positively broken and a shadow of who I once was. In the future, I would nurture my individuality in a relationship and encourage my partner to do the same. Being with Fred had been like being slowly buried alive, powerless to the taste and feel of dirt burning your eyes, screaming out for help while everyone watched. I try to live without regret but, when it was all said and done, I was ashamed of my behaviour while I was with Fred. However, I am proud I could still breathe when I finally stood up. Fred would go on to tell people I broke off our engagement, yet fail to mention there had been no yes to begin with. Embarrassed by that time in my life, I was quick to explain the technicalities of choice. It was not an *engagement* ring Fred gave me, it was a *maybe* ring.

Maybe it will work better the next time around.

Guitar Love

After Fred, I took a two-year hiatus from dating and entertainment to enjoy my own company; I still had male friends but did not attempt any sort of intimacy. I'd had two proposals so I knew I was loveable *enough*, but I needed those two years to learn to love myself enough not to repeat my experience with Fred.

After two years on hiatus, I decided a grown woman has needs. Maybe I could just have a sexual relationship and have my needs met without worrying about the emotional needs of another. But the proposal that followed this decision is proof fate has a sense of humour—either that or fate is vengeful. It was the next proposal that taught me, despite everyone's best efforts, someone could be lost.

I was smack dab in the middle of my twenties, working as a karaoke DJ three nights a week and at weddings and corporate events on the weekend. It was a great job for me; I love listening to music and have always appreciated watching people dance. There is something truly spectacular about people moving for one another and communicating without words. Although karaoke isn't for everyone, from behind the controls it's magical: during the late hours of the night a quiet friend can easily become a popular singing star, and the regular at the bar who walks his day unnoticed can stand on a stage and be seen. Whether good or bad at karaoke, everyone has a chance to discover something about themselves and be applauded for doing so.

It was while working karaoke at a little bar on Main Street that I first saw Peter. He walked in with scruffy jeans, work boots, and a leather jacket. He was not a tall man but his height didn't matter after he looked at me with a naughty smile. Once he got his beer, Peter walked by me as though he had never seen me and headed straight to a woman sitting alone at the back of the bar. For weeks, this was all I knew of Peter: a walk-by who barely acknowledged my existence. *No matter*, I thought. I had already decided I only wanted my needs met, and although I wasn't certain how to go about that, I would figure it out if the moment should present itself.

After about three months, I noticed Peter started coming into the bar with a male friend instead of the woman; rumour around the bar was the two of them had split up. It may sound strange, but when I looked at Peter, he felt important. I was meant to know him, and I felt it as clearly as I could my own skin. Sometimes he would come in and sing, but he still kept to himself, until one night he asked if I wanted to hang out sometime; I don't know if it was his perfect blue eyes that made me say yes or his smile, which made his lips look like he was saying "What have you got to lose?" When I paused, he winked his left eye at me and I just had to say yes.

When I finished work that night, Peter helped me pack up the equipment and we went back to his apartment with his friend. The three of us sat around talking about music while they played video games. As morning threatened its approach, Peter asked me to follow him. We walked to the fire escape stairs at the back of the apartment and he turned to me.

"Wait a minute or so and you'll see this is the best place to watch the sunrise." He barely looked at me when he spoke.

I could tell it wasn't just a line he told girls by how fixated his eyes were on the sky while he waited patiently. I stood beside him, more interested in the man next to me than the sun that would appear. Peter was right; it was a great place to watch the sun say hello. After, I said my goodbyes, but he insisted on walking me home. I'd had fun, and could never imagine hurting a man like Peter with trashy offers.

The three of us would go on to hang out often—Peter, his friend, and me. One day Peter asked if I would like to go out during the day on a Saturday. He borrowed a car and came to pick me up, his friend in the backseat. We decided to go shopping at the sporting goods store. My apartment was very large and every large apartment needs two hockey nets; we got new sticks, gloves, and a ball to match. We played hockey all afternoon, and when we tired from our sport, Peter would pull his guitar out and play for us.

On Monday nights, I would cover the bar for the owner so she could play in her pool league. The pay was fair and it was a nice break from carrying karaoke equipment around. Peter showed up one Monday night carrying his guitar case. I asked if he wanted something to drink when he sat in front of me.

"No," he said with his perfect smile, "I just wanted you to have this. Don't worry, I'll teach you how to play." Then he lifted the case to the bar.

"Are you serious?" I asked.

Peter nodded his head. There was nothing assuming about his behaviour, it was just raw honesty.

I loved my gift, and I still couldn't shake the idea I was meant to know him. Peter had a feeling of importance, enough that I was willing to explore getting to know him better.

Peter started coming to my apartment without his friend more and more; he would teach me to play guitar and I would cook for him as payment. He was unlike anyone I had ever met; he approached with innocence and with a genuine interest in knowing me. We would talk for hours, and I took great comfort being near him. As the friendship grew stronger, we would share more and more.

Growing up as a short man had not made life easy for Peter and he spoke of his trials with the reflection and strength that helped him overcome his size. He spoke about trying to rescue a bird once and his father teaching him that sometimes you have to let things go. He talked about how his mother packed extra sandwiches for lunch at his insistence that he was still hungry at the end of the day, when the truth was he noticed another child never had a lunch and he felt compelled to share. His mother later found out the truth and continued to pack an extra sandwich for him. I had personally felt his kindness and seen how gentle he was with his friend. None of the rumours at the bar spoke of anything unkind of him and I felt completely at ease with him. I liked his stories and although he was mostly self-educated, he was brilliant, with great potential. The more I came to know Peter, the more I was convinced he could be considered a genius if he had devoted more time to his studies.

One night after the bar, Peter and his friend walked me home—a common activity. In the neighbourhood where I lived, I agreed it was for my own safety. That night, they came in so we could order food for delivery. After we ate our late night dinner, it was decided they would sleep over; I made them beds on the couch and said goodnight.

Once I was in bed, Peter hollered, "Are you really going to make me sleep out here beside the snoring guy?"

"Where else would you sleep?" I asked.

"With you," came the reply.

With you would be the words whispered gently in the dark that changed everything.

"Okay, I guess," I whispered back.

There are some moments in life you never forget. Peter walking into the room in his boxer shorts with only the moonlight shining on him was one of those moments. He may have been short but I had never seen anyone in real life with that much muscle before. I rolled over, tried not to notice, and put my back to him. He got in bed with his back facing mine. We lay like that for at least ten minutes before he rolled over and cuddled up to me. Then, gently, he rolled my head toward him and gave me a kiss only an unassuming, kind man could give: gentle, graceful—an invitation to love him back. Kissing him was the most natural feeling I had ever had. His arms were warm and I wanted to be in them.

"I don't want anything serious," I said, knowing it was already too late for that. He only responded with a kiss—not another word was spoken that night. We moved gently with discovery; it was where we were meant to be. There was a sense of relief, like fate was watching us with approval. By morning, it was clear we were more than friends, and I was positive someone who felt that good must be meant to be. Everything about us felt right in its perfect place.

I don't think I knew I loved Peter until after about a month of us carrying on. It was a Saturday night. Peter came into the bar as usual but stood behind me, leaning against the wall. His guitar was on the floor at his feet along with a bag, and without as much as a word he pulled his beer to his lips to take a drink.

"What's with the bag?" I inquired.

"I'm leaving in an hour; I took a job an hour out of town." He did not make eye contact with me when he spoke.

"I see," I said, trying to keep my composure. "You ever coming back?" I felt entitled to know, and thought it was odd he had never mentioned anything until right before he was about to leave.

Peter's naughty smile came across his face and he winked. "You can visit me too, you know."

It was not his words that reassured me about our relationship; it was the smile and the wink. I could never imagine a day where I wouldn't want to see either. When I agreed to visit, I meant it—no game face. I wanted my life to move in the same direction as his for a while. I wanted to learn his importance.

Peter came to visit me every other weekend. When he was not by my side, we spent hours on the phone. Two months after he moved away, I found out I was pregnant—fate playing her cards. I was afraid to tell him, but when I uttered the words, his face filled with love and he ran across the room to hug my belly. He carried on about how excited he was; he had always wanted children. I hadn't been clear about what I wanted to do until that very moment, when I looked down at him on his knees, filled with joy. I thought, *I couldn't pick a better person to be the father of my child*. Peter was smart, kind, and giving. He had a good father and mother, and he wanted a child.

It was hard to tell my parents, and even harder to tell his. It was not until I was pregnant that I found out he had not spoken to his parents in five years. Given how often he mentioned them, it didn't occur to me that was the reality. We made our way to his hometown to make the introductions, and his parents were as he had described: hard working people trying to make life better for their children.

It's a strange thing to meet your boyfriend's parents for the first time when you are carrying his child, but there was no discomfort; they went out of their way to see to it that I felt a part of the family. His parents were charming and fun to be around. It all just felt like it was meant to be; I loved him, and I was proud of our soon-to-be family.

The next natural step was to move in with each other and make ourselves a home. We decided it was best I move to his town, given that he worked all week and I only worked four nights a week and still had a place to stay while I was there. We got a little apartment downtown with two bedrooms. He painted the baby's room yellow and hand-made little flowers to trim the walls. I would go back to work on Thursdays, sleeping on a friend's couch, and would come home on Sundays.

Setting up a home changes people. Living together, even if only for four days a week, will reveal anyone's true nature. It was no different for us than anyone else. We started living together with me loving *him*, and him loving the *idea* of a baby and a woman in the home. The signs that the idea was the allure more so than the relationship were slow to take hold, like painkillers administered so you don't notice them cutting your leg off; the sedation wears off and you start piecing together how you got there, wondering *why*, *how*, *when*, then *why* again. Puzzled, looking for a crutch.

Gestation and the Open Womb

It takes nine months to grow a baby—just enough time for a woman to adjust to the coming changes. Peter and I had only been living together for two months when I started feeling the structure of the relationship might not be what I had thought it would be. I continued to work until my due date, carrying DJ equipment every Thursday to Sunday, and when I was home, I spent my time tending the house until Peter came home from work. I would have dinner ready in hopes we would eat together and talk. I loved talking to him, and with my body experiencing so many changes, I wanted to share with him even more. But Peter explained that when he got home from work he didn't want to talk; he needed to be left alone. This became the routine: I would clean, cook dinner, and then watch him roll a joint. He would go outside to smoke it then come back inside and play guitar all night. As I like my personal time as well, I didn't catch on that he was avoiding me.

When I went to work, I would come home Sundays to a very messy apartment—wrappers from take-out, and evidence he was drinking and smoking pot in the house. It took two months before I brought these things to his attention; until then I just picked up after him. When I came home late on Sundays I was too tired to care, and Monday morning he would be gone to work and I didn't care much to sit in filth all day. However, after two months I'd had enough. One Monday morning, I let the filth hang around as I sat and tried to decipher how he spent the weekend without me, dissecting the evidence left lying around the apartment, until he came home.

I waited until he sat down to roll his joint before I asked, "Don't you want to pick up the garbage before you do that?" I was calm and it seemed to me to be a rather fair question.

"That's your job," he said sternly, like he meant it and was mad because I had not already cleaned it up for him.

"Are you mad I didn't clean this up for you?" I asked incredulously. That initiated our first argument on what would become a very popular topic for us: responsibilities of a home.

"You're the girl." He said it like I wasn't knocked up with a heightened sense of my gender.

"Hey, we don't live in the fifties. I pay half the bills and I am not your maid by virtue of my gender!"

Then he said it—probably the most honest reason he stuck around: "Do you forget who you were when I met you? You're lucky I'm around, so you will clean my fucking mess and every other mess without complaining!"

Who did he think I was when we met? Who did he think I was now?

"If you want a maid, you can pay me! If you like the fifties then you pay all the fucking bills and I'll stop complaining!"

Peter quickly set things straight. "I'm not paying for shit and your lazy ass can learn to clean!"

After that, there was no more to say—what could possibly follow those words? I had just moved my whole life to be with him, the kind man, and all those words were hiding inside him. How was it possible? How could that be what he was thinking—that I should be grateful for him and those words?

With nothing left to say, I packed a bag with my fresh pay in my pocket and headed to the door. Peter had already gone outside to smoke his joint.

As I passed him, he said, "Where are you going?"

Coldly, I replied, "That is none of your business anymore." I headed to the bus station, only to find out the next bus home was not until morning.

It was a brisk night. I headed to a park over the bridge that had a nice garden and I sat along the river. I knew no one in town and it was late enough that the city bus had stopped running. The flowers smelled good and the river made the night air feel colder. I thought the sound of the water might calm me down while I got a game plan together. What I knew was that the man I was now living with was harsh, unloving, and dismissive. I knew that, for the first time in my life, flight was complicated due to the new member of the family. I got scared; *could I be a single mother?* I sat on that bench in the middle of the night under an oak tree and realized there was nowhere else to go, and that I believed, as a mother, I had to exhaust all possibilities before flight; it was not just my body changing, it was my every instinct.

I walked back to the apartment slowly, trying to figure out if there was another way. When I walked in, hours later, Peter's eyes looked up as I silently passed him and went and slept in the baby's room. I had decided that my plan would be to stay in the baby's room for the short term, until I came up with a new plan.

After that fateful night, when Sundays came and I walked through the door, there was a great deal less filth lying around the apartment. I would walk Peter to the bus every day to see him off to work; he did not kiss me goodbye, but it felt like the only time he spent with me. There were other brief moments when it felt like I had him back, times when he would trace the outline of my ever-growing body. Sometimes we would go to the bar to play pool and he would sing karaoke.

When I was four months pregnant, Peter waited until we were sitting at the bus station before he told me he was changing things.

"I took a different shift at work. I start on Monday working three to eleven," he advised.

I was devastated; how would that work? "For how long?" I asked.

"Forever," he said as the bus pulled up.

"But when our kid starts school you'll never see us," I pleaded, as the extra emotions were starting to take effect.

"That's not my problem," was all he said before the door to the bus closed and carried everyone on their way.

I stood there for a few moments in the rain before I made my way home.

I had truly believed Peter cared before he told me otherwise. Even then, I still wasn't confident if the real him was the harsh man running away on a bus or the man full of joy who loved his family. When we spoke, I didn't know if *he* knew who he was. He would make rational arguments for his behaviour and we would come to a compromise. I sat on the bed at five months pregnant and he told me there was no excuse for my weight, I was not pregnant in my ass. At seven months pregnant, I sat on the bed depressed about my shape.

"I am fat and ugly, everyone is going to be saying it soon," I moped.

Peter kissed my forehead and said, "They will not, 'cause they'll have to get through me first."

The moments and days were never consistent to one personality.

At eight months pregnant, I was walking home, carrying six bags from the grocery store alone, and thought, *This is crazy, why am I walking, at eight months pregnant, this long a distance to buy and bring food to someone who won't help at all?* I attended all my doctor's visits with my mother or alone. Lamaze classes I took alone, and since he worked afternoons I was in bed before he got home and spent my days trying to be quiet for him.

At nine months pregnant, I called him at work to explain I had a severe craving for McDonald's greased-up food; he had to pass there on the way home, could he please go through the drive-thru for me? He came home empty-handed, and although he had a car now, I had to take a taxi to get there—he did not want to encourage me to get any fatter.

My due date came and went. No one prepared me for that—I had agreed to that date—and I was bitter every extra day I spent pregnant. Ten days later, my water broke in a big, disgusting mess—our child was late enough that it'd had a bowel movement in the womb. When they say *water* breaks, you expect it to look like that, water. That was not at all the case and I was revolted with my own body.

I waited until I thought most of the water was out before I headed to the hospital. Once settled into the bed, my contractions started to become more prevalent; it was a strange pain, not so much a hurt as a discomfort in the beginning. I asked Peter if he could hold my hand for a minute, and he put his hand out reluctantly.

"There's no need to make a big deal out of this," he stated.

"Out of what, my body morphing to spit your kid out?" I retorted.

All I could think was, *I hope today is not going to be one of those days.*

When the contractions passed, I went for a walk alone, and when I returned to the room, Peter was asleep on a chair. I crawled into bed and fell asleep as well. The doctor woke me up in the morning to tell me she was bringing me to the delivery room; I was not fully dilated, but our child's heartbeat was fluctuating.

Our child made a safe appearance with a perfectly round head full of hair. Nothing before that moment mattered anymore; the room was full of love and I was hell-bent on making my family work. We would have to find a way; our child was worth every ounce of our energy. I readily admit I never wanted children, but I knew from the first time I held my baby I had only thought that because I had not met my child yet.

A Rising Shrill

After having a baby, a natural change occurs in your perspective of time. The moments holding and loving a child make it impossible to keep with the natural order of the clock-ticking world. Everything begins to be measured by the age of a child, and how old you were when that milestone occurred in their life. It is not a conscious change but rather an evolution of purpose. The same could be said for Peter and me; our whole world was about the baby and I was hard pressed to remember who I was prior to giving birth, like my old self left my body upon ejecting the baby, and all that was left of me were the parts designed for loving my dear child. That great love and purpose blinded me to Peter's struggles, but after the first year of our child's life, I knew time would not play in our favour. The relationship was toxic despite my best efforts; unsettling fights about house cleaning and my body were a frequent and common occurrence. My every attempt to avoid confrontation was somehow foiled, and nothing was ever good enough.

When our child was around four months of age, Peter called me to the kitchen.

"I want to show you how to make a proper sandwich," he said.

Although my recent sleep deprivation made me instantly intolerant of the conversation, I did not interject—I was curious just how far it would go. Slowly, Peter opened the bread bag, all the while explaining in great detail how to do so: "First you see, you have to remove this little clip, then slowly open the front of the bag, reach in, and pull out a slice of bread."

I was astonished at what was occurring, but even more so, I was curious as to what part of my sandwich-making had inspired such a heated demonstration. If the tutorial was unavoidable, I might as well learn from it.

Peter continued, "Only after that do you pull out the meat, THEN grab two slices of cheese..." It was the cheese. It must be, given the emphasis he gave it. Somehow, I had not placed the cheese slices on the bread properly. "You have to put the cheese slice on, ensuring the bottom of the slice touches the very bottom edge of the bread. It would be stupid not to do that. It would make no sense, why would anyone do such a stupid thing?"

How he looked at me when he said *stupid* made my tiredness very relevant. I raised my eyebrows to acknowledge his point and began to walk away. He wasn't done.

"Wait," Peter continued with a laugh, "because this isn't a stupid sandwich, you have to not be lazy and take it a step further—you need to cut the second slice of cheese in just the right spot, so it fits perfectly and gives full coverage to the bread. Do you think you can handle that? Do you think I can stop having fucking pathetic, stupid sandwiches in my lunch now?"

I started to laugh, I could not believe what I was hearing or seeing. *He must think I am stupid if he feels the need to show me how to make a sandwich*, I thought, *extremely stupid if he's comfortable speaking to me this way*.

"Why are you laughing?" Peter asked with disgust.

"Well you see," I began to explain, "I think that when someone takes the time to make you a sandwich at all you just say *thank you*." My emphasis was a warning as to how resentful I was at being woken up for his seminar. "Now, I understand you are remarkable at making a non-stupid sandwich and that is what you would appreciate from now on. So the only possible thing I can do now to help you be happy is to just let you use your *brilliant* skills every day and make your own sandwich. That way you'll make yourself, and me, happy!"

Peter muttered something after me about how that was a lazy person's response and how I didn't like taking directions, but I continued my walk to bed and pretended I couldn't hear him.

That was the day I officially stopped preparing Peter's lunch for work. It was not what he was trying to show me, but it was most certainly the way in which he did that stopped me from trying to get it right.

Most of the time Peter and I lived on different schedules; I would be up all day with the baby, he would wake up around one in the afternoon. From one to two thirty he would exercise, smoke a joint, take a shower, then make a perfect sandwich. He mentioned on more than one occasion that this was not mine or the baby's time with him, it was his personal time. After his routine, he would leave for work, and I would wait up for him to have dinner together when he returned home. He arrived at eleven thirty at night and would go straight to roll and smoke a joint, then sit to have dinner. After dinner, he would play guitar all night, because as he pointed out, that was also his personal time. In fact, he found it to be a nuisance to have company over for dinner as well. I stopped waiting up for him not long after.

We lived like two roommates who only cared about one another when we'd had too much to drink. Peter seemed happy about the baby and me when other people were around; an audience made him behave like the man I knew before I was pregnant. An audience made him attentive and loving, almost happy, although we fought prior to every public appearance. The fights sometimes made me forget the event; other times, I would insist we go. When I insisted, I would have to do so despite his objections, until it was impossible for us to make it on time. After a while, I caught on to this and began lying about our departure time, giving myself two hours of leeway. It was as if playing the part of a good man was too much effort for Peter, and I should feel privileged that he would join us.

I was becoming passive-aggressive trying to fight the crazy to survive. You could almost see the old Peter wrestle with the ugly Peter that was trying to take over, and I was always happy to see the old Peter emerge and fight his way back to civilization. We would celebrate with laughter, without mention of the ugly Peter standing in the shadows, waiting for the stage light to fade. Looking back, I know the old Peter was scared of the ugly Peter, but we never talked about it in hopes of not disrupting the happiness that the old Peter would bring. The air was so fragile with old Peter, and we both worked hard not to invite the negativity back.

Fourteen months after having the baby, my love for old Peter was evident when the doctor announced to me that another child would soon make its way into our world, onto the infected stage we called a home—I performed the role of Mother while Peter tried to decide on a character.

The more fate played its card, the more Peter felt out of control, until control was not had by anyone. I started to hear the whispers and echoes of people around us, looking upon the child and me as victims. The ugly Peter's fierce voice was more and more evident, and it became difficult to explain to those around us that the old Peter was still around. I knew he wasn't, but knew how everyone would worry if they learned the truth. The man I knew, the father of my children, was with us less and less.

It's interesting how in my relationship with Fred I became lost, and now it was Peter who was lost, not to me, but to himself. We would talk about mental health in hopes of being able to get him help, but the behaviour was always someone else's fault, not his. Mostly it was my fault, or so I was told. The lectures and seminars continued. I wanted the old Peter back, and the promising family that was offered with him.

    I held on to that dream for as long as I could; trying to give their best to the children, parents exhaust all possibilities before giving up. It took me a long time to accept that his cruelty could not be cured; it may have been there all along. I was always holding onto a dream, afraid of the nightmare. It was a Saturday when I woke up to the truth. The eldest child and I were at the table eating breakfast and I was eight months pregnant. Peter came storming into the house after smoking his joint, screaming about the disaster of our home. I heard him speak and I looked around to see that the mess he was describing only existed in his head. You cannot compete with that. What could I possibly say that would make our realities the same? I stood and tried to pull our child out of the chair quickly to get it away from the danger. My child, almost two years of age, stood at my side, shaking and holding my hand ever so tight. He was standing, screaming in my face, when I heard our child's little courageous voice say, "The house is clean."

The look on Peter's face was not shock; it was emotionless, terrifying.

"We will go upstairs. You stay away from us until you calm down," I said in my best attempt to distract him from our child's words. I began to hustle us up the stairs, but I heard his heavy footsteps following as we reached the top landing.

"Quick, go to the room and shut the door, sweetie," I said, panicking when I felt his hand on my shoulder, turning me around.

Before I knew what was happening, I felt his fist hit the side of my face. I was not overwhelmed with pain or fear, just anger. The look on his face was clear: the punch was what he needed to snap out of his fit, but I no longer cared.

"You just punched your pregnant girlfriend in front of your two-year-old child. Do you feel like a man now?" I thought it was fair to ask, although I was mostly trying to make a point. Peter started to cry but did not reply. I stood and watched for my own satisfaction.

"I think it best that when you leave today, you don't ever come back!" I said, and I meant it.

Peter left and did not come back for three days. I spent those three days feeling ashamed that I would soon be at a hospital, giving birth alone with a two-year-old beside me. I knew I could never afford to care for the children without him. Maybe he could change if he were to get help; there were community organizations that could assist.

When Peter came back home he begged for forgiveness, reassuring me it would never repeat itself. We put a game plan in place: both of us would attend marriage counselling and he would seek out professional help for himself. I reminded him that I loved him and I believed in him, and I truly believed that together we could bring joy back to our home.

A month later, we gave birth to our second child. Having a new baby at home made peace appear for us again. The joy was around just long enough to leave Peter delusional about not needing help. By the time the youngest was two months old, Peter's behaviour was everyone else's fault again. We had just bought our first home so I was too preoccupied to notice him changing our game plan. By the time we moved into our home, there was little chance for a recovery mission to find the old Peter; the move confirmed that all we now had were two beautiful kids, a home, and one cruel Peter with no hope. I was living in the aftermath of defeated hope and soon found myself plotting how to get across enemy lines.

Armanda Lambert

The Cursed Home

We were settled in our new home for a week before I found out it was cursed. Peter and I were again living as roommates, hardly crossing paths, when my new neighbour approached to introduce herself. She was a very kind woman who had lived beside our new home for many years. She was an extremely talented gardener, and her property looked like it belonged in a fairy tale. She explained to me that the man who'd had our house built was a very cranky man, and she could not hide her distaste for him when she spoke; she said it was his fault the house was cursed. She had noticed no one ever lived in the house for more than two and a half years before everything fell apart. The people who lived there before us had gone bankrupt. The people before them were divorced. The couple before them had to sell due to a death, and on and on her story went. She asked if I had noticed anything strange, but aside from Peter, I could not say that I had. I kept thinking that maybe, like in our case, the residents' situations were already falling apart before anyone took possession.

One day, Peter came home from work only an hour after he had left.

"I quit my job, so you better think of a way to make more money, and fast!" he said with no remorse.

"What do you mean, you quit?" I asked.

"What don't you understand? I quit!"

"What's your plan?" I inquired.

"I'm going back into labour jobs," he said before going into his room to roll a joint. Apparently, I needed no other explanation and it was clear he was not turning back on his actions.

That night, Peter left the house without notice while I was putting the kids to bed. I sat wondering where he might be as the night progressed, and wondered if he was coming back. I wondered if his time off work meant that he would seek out help or make him calmer. The phone rang around midnight, waking me up from my sleep on the couch.

"Hello?"

"It's me," Peter said, clearly having had too many drinks.

"Where are you?" I asked, worried if he was alright.

"I'm at the "'rippers, drinking," he said shamelessly, before he continued. "I'm watching all these girls take their clothes off and I was thinking you would be mad." He was clearly past his limit.

"When are you coming home?" I asked sternly.

"Will you marry me?" he asked.

Knowing he was very drunk, I did not assume he meant it or would remember saying it. "What? Are you proposing marriage over the phone from a stripper bar?" I asked in horror.

"Yes, I guess I am! So what do you say?" he pressed on as he began to laugh.

Here I was, on proposal number three, and all I could think of to say was "Come home!" before I hung up in disgrace.

Peter's proposal would not be the only one I would receive over the phone, yet it seemed past due, given that we already owned a home together and had two children. Was it possible he meant it, despite his condition? If he did, it would need to be readdressed. I would have to give it serious consideration. Did I want to be married to this man? He was the father of my children and that was the reason I was still trying to make our relationship work. That is what I am told marriage is: two people working for the common goal of a family. Is that what we were, two people trying to make the best of the bed we'd made? The children had made our relationship like an arranged marriage, and for good or bad, we were now in it. We were considered married under the eyes of the law anyway, what difference would it be to make it official? Maybe with time and work we could turn our arrangement into love again. I did love him in the beginning and now I loved him through our children. The kids were both healthy and strong, so maybe I could nurture us to be the same.

  I over-thought Peter's proposal. I know because the next morning there was no mention of it. Peter did not bring it up again while we were together. He carried on the next day with the same cold disposition that had become our way of life, reaffirming to me the only correct answer I would have: no, marrying Peter would only allow him to believe his behaviour was acceptable and help was not desperately needed.

  Three days later, I had plans to go home and visit family and friends. Peter preferred to drop me off rather than to join me; I preferred the same. We had no issues getting to my mother's house; he was good at pretending he cared when others were around. He said goodbye and I settled the children into my parents' home. On the first night, my father was out late so my mother and I sat up watching movies. First a children's movie, then together my mother and I bathed and tucked them into bed with stories. We continued our movie spree afterward with good snacks and something a little more appropriate for our ages. It was calm; I was not worried about an unexpected fit of rage. The only drama was what we would witness in the film. I thought about how ashamed my family would be about my life, despite that I still felt in control. I truly believed it was only affecting me and not my children.

When I went to bed, I thought about my neighbour and her stories of curses. Was it the house's fault Peter had gotten worse, or was the onset of his mental condition caused by his age? Was it simply that he felt out of control and that's what brought his true nature out? I concluded it was not the house because Peter could control it; he could be kind and understand social expectations if there was an audience. He could apply the same techniques when he was around us, he just *chose* not to. I decided Peter's proposal was not a real one because he did not respect me or his own children if he could not bring social order home with him. However, I don't rule out the curse of the house— I received two proposals within one week and was introduced to my fifth prospective proposer while I was living there. My perspective on life and expectations changed drastically in that home.

That Saturday night at my mother's I had made plans to have dinner with Evan, the boy I punched when I was young, and Rex, a common friend I had known for ages. My father and mother would care for the children and had no expectation of what time I should be home.

Evan picked me up in his car, which was very amusing to me as he never drove while I lived in town. Him driving made me feel like he was an adult now and it was strange to be reminded about the time that had passed. We spoke in the car about his work, and how he was doing. Evan had been in my life for everything, including the kids' baby showers, and he had taken some time to visit with them before we left the house. He adored children and had always wanted his own. The children's fondness for him was evident in the giggles and joy that filled the room during his visit. I made a point of telling him how pleased I was to see him happy and put together before we parked the car at the restaurant.

Rex was waiting outside with a big smile on his face. Rex is a man of great principle and I am always overjoyed to see him. It was a rare occasion for us all to be together again, like the good old days. I gave him a hug, because I have a selfish side that always needs a hug from Rex; I don't know why, but his hugs always leave me feeling loved and cared for. Rex had a family, two children with his high school sweetheart, and I thought how blessed he was to have found love so easily, and to be so confident in it that his wife would hold his love for all time.

It was nice to be with Evan and Rex over dinner; it reminded me what normal life was like. The conversations were good, covering the good old days and how much all of our lives had changed. After dinner, we said our farewells. Evan and I got in the car, ready to head back to my parents.

Evan turned to me and said, "Are you in a rush or do you want to hang out a little longer?"

"Where do you want to go?" I asked, not certain what he was offering.

He just smiled and said, "We're not too old to hit the town." He laughed and started the car.

"I'm in," was all I said as I laughed at how right he was. I was excited; it had been far too long since I'd had a night out. It would be fun to see how the nightlife in town had changed since I'd left.

First, we stopped at a karaoke bar so he could sing. I had no idea Evan was a singer, and he was very good at it. He had a natural stage presence and, surprisingly, a very good voice. We sat at a table with some of the regulars he knew, mostly adoring women who were curious about who I was. They were fun, and they told me stories about the Evan they all loved, and I felt a little naughty listening without him knowing what we were discussing. I shared stories with them about him when he was younger—that made them love him even more.

Afterward, Evan and I headed to a different bar downtown where we could sit and talk without his fan club listening. It was a little Irish pub where everyone was too busy drinking to care about two people sitting in a corner. That's where my fourth proposal happened. First, it came with a big dose of reality.

"Look, I know you say you're happy," Evan started, "but I don't believe you." It was gentle enough, like he was heading into a conversation of concern.

"What do you mean?" I asked, trying to feel out where he was going.

"Peter does not love you and he is never going to marry you! If he was going to, he would have done so already. I love you; I always have. Marry me!"

I was in shock. Evan didn't know Peter had just asked me to marry him three days prior from a bar. Surprisingly, these were words I always thought I would hear from Evan, what my childhood heart fantasized about hearing. I had always believed we were meant to be, but Evan's timing was wrong.

"We've never even had sex," was all I could say.

"I'm sure we would figure that out. If we're bad at it at first we could just keep trying...together." Evan answered like he had been prepared for my reaction.

"How would you be happy? I would be the unfaithful woman who left her husband for you!" I replied. I was feeling anxious; I knew I was considering.

"I would be happy for the rest of my life knowing I was the man you left your husband for," he replied calmly, but he was looking more and more insecure.

"You don't mean it," I protested.

"Yes I do," he replied.

"Stop it, how could you say these things to me? How could I ever have you near my family knowing you are just standing on the sidelines waiting for me to fail so you can pick up the pieces? You are only asking me to make your mom happy, but this is not the right way to do it. I want to go home!" I exclaimed. I was overwhelmed and at a serious crossroads. I was exploring what I was truly capable of.

"I'll take you home, and you can say any reason you want for why I ask. But I love you, and that is why I am asking," Evan stated. With that, he stood up and put his coat on, and still, he reached his hand out to help me up.

We drove to my parents' house in silence and Evan got out and walked me to the door. Before I opened it, he gave me a hug.

"Pick me. Love me. Be my wife," he whispered in my ear. I nearly cried as I rushed into the house.

I had trouble sleeping that night and I decided the house's curse must be temptation. I was tempted to take his offer; it was an easy way out. It was an expected result of the long history Evan and I had. One that would not shock either of our families. Evan's and my history were intrinsically intertwined, even beyond church talent shows and schoolyard bloody noses.

When I was fourteen, I received a phone call from Rex. He had me on speakerphone; I could tell by the annoying background noises.

"I want to set you up on a blind date," he said.

"No thank you," I responded quickly.

"Why not?" he asked, shocked, like he thought I was desperate to date someone.

"Because we're young; anyone who can't get their own date at this age is not a person I care to date," I responded, annoyed with the conversation.

"But he is perfect for you; trust me," Rex replied.

I was neither convinced nor entertained and quickly let him go.

Two days later, I was walking home and could see Rex sitting on my front porch with a boy beside him. The boy had exquisite blue eyes and a strong build. I approached, trying not to show my interest, afraid of looking uncool.

"Hey, what are you doing here?" I asked once I was close enough. Rex hadn't told me he was coming over and there he was, with company.

"I wanted to introduce you to Evan, the guy you said was pathetic if he needed to be set up on a blind date," Rex replied with great pleasure. Both of them smiled.

I instantly turned red with embarrassment as I watched Evan's eyes look me over. He was even cuter when he smiled; he had a smile that would make even his worst enemy smile back.

Evan spoke for the first time.

"Did you go to a French school?" he asked.

Quickly it came back to me. There he stood, fourteen years old, the boy who had irritated me at the church, the boy whom I'd given a bloody nose to at school. He was crossing my path again. Fate had brought him there.

I invited them both in. Evan was polite and not annoying. He was funny and kind. He was charming, and my family loved him.

From that day on, Evan was a part of my life. I spent every day with Rex and Evan. I would often come home from school and find him having tea with my mother. Saturday mornings I would wake up to find him waiting for me to snuggle on the couch to watch cartoons. We would go to school dances together as friends and he would say, "Look at my bubble butt," as he shook his fanny in my direction. He was always very fun. Evan dated all my friends while we hung out every day. I was always nervous knocking on Evan's door because his older brother would answer the door and give me a look like I was doing something wrong, then announce with a devilish tone, "Your *friend* is here."

Quickly it became clear that Evan, Rex, and I were more than friends—we were family. On Valentine's Day, Evan and Rex put their money together to buy me roses and chocolate. Together they taught me how to play pool, and I always knew we had each other's backs. We first drank alcohol together and held private meetings about each other if we worried about a change in behaviour. If any of us were sick in the hospital, we were there together. When Rex first started talking about the girl who would eventually be his wife, we watched him build the courage to speak to her. We were the courage that bullied him into asking her on a date, honestly, because we were sick of him talking about her. In our teens, Evan and I never crossed that line, though. The progression of our friendship was at the forefront of our thoughts, but never something we verbalized to each other.

When I left for university in second year, Evan's mother drove me the seven hours away from home. When I came home that Christmas, Evan and I went out on the town. We danced all night, making jokes about our bubble butts. We finished the night at my parents' house. It was not uncommon for Evan to sleep over; he had been doing it for years.

That night, before he went into my sister's old room to sleep, he turned and kissed me goodnight. It was a nice kiss and the first romantic affection he had ever shown me on a physical level. I didn't know what to make of it.

"Well, goodnight," I said, raising my eyebrows.

Evan smiled; he had finally showed me he was a man.

"Goodnight to you," he responded with a proud smile. Then he went into the room, leaving the door slightly open.

I started to walk to my room, but turned back with the intent to ask him about the kiss. I could see through the crack of the door his reflection in the mirror: he was already undressing for bed, so I changed my mind—best not to interrupt.

I'm not proud of what happened next, but my pride doesn't change what happened. I stood there and watched as Evan undressed. I had never seen him shirtless before; I thought I just wanted to see that. But once his shirt was off, I stayed. I had meant to leave, but he started undoing his pants and I found myself paralyzed, knowing no one would ever know if I stood there a little longer, looking. When his pants were off he slowly put his hands to tuck his thumbs into the edge of his boxers, as if he was about to take them off. I knew I should've walked away, but if this was a fight or flight moment at hand, I was still making up my mind to react. He pulled them down slightly, and then looked straight at me through the mirror, as if he knew I had been there the entire time. I had been caught. He turned his body to look straight at me, smiled, and gently said goodnight again as if sending me on my way. I raced back to my room as quickly as the rhythm of my heart, trying to think of the excuses I would use in the morning to explain my behaviour.

The next morning, Evan was on the couch waiting for me to watch cartoons, and the reality of the moment that had passed settled in. We were both only home a week from school; there was no sense trying to start anything up. Instead, we maintained our friendship. Although it was rare for us to see each other in person, I always had a special place in my heart for Evan.

Now, years later, I found myself considering what forever would feel like with Evan. I knew he would be an exceptional father, and he had always been a good friend to me. I imagined we could work out the details of intimacy, as he had suggested, but none of that changed the circumstances with Peter, who had proposed three days before, over the phone, from a bar.

I woke up Sunday morning feeling defeated. My father was eating breakfast with the kids.

"You okay?" he asked, as if I were wearing my shame like a red, obscenely flashy dress that hurt his eyes to look at.

"Yeah, why do you ask?" I replied defensively.

"Fun night, I guess," he said sarcastically.

I made myself a bowl of cereal. I wanted to tell him about what had happened, but how could I admit that I had considered leaving the father of my young children? The reasons would be painful for him to hear and for me to say aloud. Could I explain the reasons why I thought it would work better in a different home? Childhood crush, fantasy?

"Are you positive there's nothing you want to talk about?" He asked in such a way I knew I should be curious why, but before I could speak, he continued. "Do you know that people get nose bleeds from high blood pressure, especially when they are experiencing stress?"

With those words, I knew why he was asking. I could feel the blood dripping down my face, as if summoned by his words. I quickly ran to the bathroom mirror for proof and he followed me to help tend to my Pinocchio nose.

"So it was a good night?" he repeated.

I confessed everything about the night before, like he was the sheriff and I was making a case to get away with murder. "What am I going to do? I don't want to lose the friendship, but how can I have him around Peter knowing how he feels? All the time he was supporting me, was he just waiting for me to fail?

Now I should rip my life apart because he is impatient?"

I carried on with the pace of a toddler having a tantrum as if somehow my father was responsible for my heartache. I cried for hours looking around my house, knowing every corner and crack held a part of Evan's and my history. I cried because I knew Peter was on his way to pick us all up and take us home. I cried because I knew I did not want to get in the car with him, but I would have to. I cried lying to my children about why I was crying, out of fear they would tell their father. I cried mostly because I wanted to be the girl Evan wanted me to be, but I knew that was not where I was meant to be. I knew it was not our destiny and I would be a mistake for Evan.

When I calmed slightly, I called him, thinking maybe he had forgotten he'd said it. Maybe it was a bad joke he was playing. I called him because I knew when I said no it changed our friendship forever, and I wanted him to know I was mourning the details already.

The phone rang three times; I didn't know if I would leave a message or not, but he finally picked up.

"Are you calling to marry me yet?" were the first words out of his mouth.

"I can't marry you; it's not what you want. You deserve better." I was trying to be honest with him as gently as I could be.

"That is not the answer I want," he uttered before he hung up.

With that, our history was altered, and maturity finally had. Fate and temptation had tested me and I was the weaker one, sitting on a couch trying to get my game face back before Peter arrived.

He arrived late, as he tended to do, anxious to get us all in the car. I could tell Peter was having a bad day by his demeanour, and by how aggressively he packed the children into the vehicle. I gave my love to my parents for helping me through the weekend and after kisses were had, I turned to leave.

As I reached for the door handle, I knew what fate I was accepting and what dream I was leaving behind. I also knew my silence was better than the truth to avoid hurting anyone further. I got into the car knowing Peter was not aware of what had transpired, and I buckled up to go back to our cursed home.

I entered the car for safe passage and quickly realized we were just his prisoners; Peter buckled up ready to deliver a seminar and happy that the car would act as a dungeon that prevented us from not listening—prevented us from seeking shelter from his words. Our seatbelts acted as carefully placed shackles. Only his hand with the keys could free us then.

Shylock Converses with Portia

Peter pulled away from my parents' home as if someone had dropped a chequered flag and we were the underdogs in the race. He weaved through traffic like the other vehicles were a nuisance.

"Peter, what is wrong?" I asked halfway home, when the speed he was driving at became alarming.

"We need to talk," he said, and I instantly feared he might have heard about Evan.

"What about? Slow down the car; we can talk," I implored.

Peter looked through me as if I had not spoken. When he was in a mood, his entire face would change: his eyes would become black and his face would become red while the veins in his neck appeared like tree roots. He didn't look at me even when eye to eye, as if he was possessed and his eyes were hands reaching out to grab my neck. That was how he looked when he began to speak.

"I am going to start a business!" he proclaimed.

"That's great! Why are you mad?" I inquired.

"Why? Well, I have a dream. Did you ever read *The Merchant of Venice*?" he asked.

It was as if whatever had control of his mind was new to expressing ideas; the sentence was so jumpy I just sat and stared at him with confusion.

"Did you read *The Merchant of Venice*?" he screamed, like I had hesitated too long before answering.

"Yes, in high school. Why?" I asked. *Why* is what I asked but *why* is still unclear to me to this day.

"Because I have a dream," Peter seethed. His anger was mounting.

"What is the dream and why are we talking about a Shakespeare play?" I asked. Peter's driving was still erratic and I thought that if he could just answer that question everything would calm down.

"Shylock had a dream; he wanted his pound of flesh. Portia is the only reason he did not get his revenge. I have a dream and I am going to start this business and if you think that you or those kids are going to stop me..." He paused for dramatic effect.

"Well, if you try to get in my way, don't think for a second I won't get my pound of flesh!"

I started to cry; my ears hurt from what I was hearing and my heart wept for the dream I'd just left behind. I cried for my parents, who had raised me better than to end up in this situation. I was grateful the children were not old enough to understand his words, but I was restless knowing I could not run them to safety.

"What are you crying for?" Peter mocked. "I will get my pound of flesh unless you and the kids stay the fuck out of my way!" There was no remorse in his words, none at all.

"Are you threatening me and the children? What does that mean, when you say 'a pound of flesh'?" My words were aggressive because I had nothing left to lose; my rage did not leave time for him to answer. "I asked you a question! If I get in the way, what happens to the children and me? What is it you need to say to me?" My eyes fixated on Peter to watch his physical response to my words. I may have loved the old Peter, but the new Peter had fully taken over now. This Peter was talking like a sociopath. Maybe if I stared at him while he responded I would be able to assess the level of risk.

"I am saying staying out of my way is what is best for you!" He said it as if I was hard of understanding.

"You're saying it wasn't a threat?" I pressed.

"It is not a threat, it is a warning," he responded cowardly, sensing my anger.

"Well if it's not a threat, I don't have to care; I don't have to listen to you at all!" I was cavalier in my words to test him. Peter did not face me; he just stared at the road in silence and took us home.

That night when I went to bed, I heard Peter talking downstairs. I got out of bed to see if he was on the phone with someone—it would have been comforting if he had been. Instead, from the stairs, I watched him walk around the kitchen—a knife in hand—talking to himself with his black eyes. The words did not matter to me; I went back to bed and fought to stay awake to monitor his movements.

In the morning, Peter finally came upstairs, unarmed, and crawled into bed. I rose and got the children and I dressed for the day, and Michael came by to pick us up and we all went for coffee. When Peter had been working he had introduced me to Michael, a man he worked with whom I became instantly fond of. We became closer and closer over time as Peter seemed not to mind our friendship; if anything he even encouraged it. I did not shelter Michael from the truth;

I told him about my proposals, so close together, about the knife, and the car ride. I explained how both proposals came with beer breath, from two different people, and how one forgot he said it and the other refused to stop remembering. Peter would later tell me he meant his proposal, quoting back the wording like it was not crass. "I even offered to marry you," he said, as if he would have been doing me a favour.

Michael looked the way I felt as I spoke. He passed no judgment. He had a policy: if you did not ask for his opinion, he would not impose it on you. He was also not overly worried, as I had also disclosed I'd called a lawyer and set up a consultation, now ready to leave the madness.

After I told him about the nosebleed, I turned to him and asked, "Is that why we're friends? Are you waiting on the sidelines for my life to fail?" Still new to our friendship I thought it best to ask.

"No," he responded with a reassuring chuckle.

"Good. My heart can't take it. I like our friendship and I don't ever want to lose it. I can't have you be *that guy* to me. Please don't ever come to me and tell me that feelings have changed. Promise me you won't be that guy, because I believe in you and I believe in us, just the way we are." It had been a crazy week and I meant every word. Being with Michael calmed me and brought joy to my life. I had already lost Evan, I was preparing to lose Peter officially, and I could not stand to lose Michael as well.

"I promise," he said in a way that I believed.

My life changed when I moved my children and me out of our home. The chaos of the outside world worked like magic to repair the strength inside my soul; I began to take care to fortify myself, and explore how it came to be so out of order. I would mourn the old Peter and wish he could understand who he'd become, but I could see the good in him every day in our kids, and I took solace in that. Once the children were asleep, I would self-reflect to try to understand my part and his part and dissect where it went wrong. I had loved a man then chose not to marry him, not because I loved him any less, but because marriage should not be accepted as a challenge to heal someone. My only choice now that my children were born was to be or not to be their mother. My only job as a mother is to keep my children safe and loved. I chose to be a mother, which meant I could not choose to stay with Peter.

Eventually I accepted that not all things could be understood. All decisions are a choice, and the only choices I had to face I have made in good faith. I said no to all four of those proposals because, in the moment the words were spoken, I knew I could not keep that commitment. Life has a way of making bends in the road and you always have a choice of where the adventure takes you. I owned my choices. My love for my children will always be greater than any ring or wedding song. I had no regret moving forward; in my heart, it was the only choice to make.

But circumstances change, and experience and perspective can make you regret words spoken, which is what I would learn in the next stage of my life.

Armanda Lambert

Survivors

Before Michael moved away, we sat together on the riverbank. He had been accepted to school and had plans to move with his girlfriend. They were both excited about their upcoming adventure, as was I about mine. We shared a can of beer over a conversation about surviving and noted that when the chips fell, we were the sort of people who always made it out clean. I pondered whether that meant we were selfish or self-preserving. We never chose the fight but we did not fall beneath it either; we did not hide, we always stood up for what was right or good from our perspective. Each of us could still stand amongst the wreckage as honest people with good intentions. I was proud of us.

Shortly after Michael left, a girlfriend of mine fell on bad luck: with obscene dramatics, her husband had ungraciously asked her to leave. She found herself homeless just as I found myself lonely without

Michael's guidance. She moved her two daughters in with me and my children. I had known her daughters since they were toddlers and there was only a little adjustment needed to have us all fit in our home. It seemed only right to help her out, but selfishly I knew I needed her there. Lola and I would make meals together for the kids and stay up all night, like young girls, solving all the problems of the world. I have been very blessed in my time with the company I keep. Some could say I had an army of women with me, all carrying their years of experience as weapons, and those people would know that Lola was the girl leading the troops.

    Lola and I carried on this way for a couple of months before the next proposal, if you were to consider it as such. You see, saying no is easy when you believe they mean it, but saying yes is even harder when you are not confident it was said at all, and you can't say anything if you are not given the chance to respond.

    Michael called on a Saturday afternoon, which was not unusual for him. He would call often to see how things were going, and I was completely indulgent; I loved his laugh and the sound of his voice. He was so wise; he always knew the right thing to say. That Saturday, however, he was in a bad mood, frustrated with how things were going lately. He complained about how everyone was offering him advice on how to live his life. He was being very harsh and aggressive with his wording, which was not at all common for him; I had never before heard him enraged. I knew he was at a crossroads.

"Everyone knows better than me apparently," he fumed.

"Well I don't know about that. I think we all just want to help you," I responded, hoping to calm him.

"You want to help?" he said sarcastically. "If you want to help me, move out here and I will give you another child!"

I heard his words and was in disbelief; I realized what he said was true. I heard him clearly—his harsh, uncensored proposal, spoken like someone had opened Pandora's box in error.

"Don't say things in anger," I insisted.

"You think anger made me say that?" he responded before he hung up the phone.

I tried to call back but he did not answer. It was months before I heard from him again; just long enough for me to start to think it was not a proposal at all. Just long enough for us to put the smokescreen back in place so our friendship could continue. Just long enough for me to lose confidence to bring it back up in conversation.

That was the fifth and last proposal to date. The proposal that appears forgotten but never responded to. The proposal I wondered if Michael ever wanted an answer to. Was he curious as to what I would have replied; was he afraid that he spoke it? A proposal, perhaps, that feared a response.

Time passed as it always does. I was playing fetch with the dog, listening to Lola and the children laughing while they played inside. I threw the ball and thought about how happy I was. I had everything I needed: happy children, playful dog—I have simple needs. In that moment, I was truly content.

Suddenly, I swore I heard my mother's weeping voice say, "My God, she is never going to get married!" I laughed aloud. I knew it was probably true; I was most likely never going to marry, but I would not say I had lost hope in the idea, no more than I would say it was never something I'd hoped for. I'd begun to believe that maybe I was fighting fate with all the suitors I had faced: every intention behind each proposal was different than the last, and although I was older and more experienced with each offer, my inner child prevailed with each answer, and I always remembered I had a choice. I always walked away with no regret in my steps.

Armanda Lambert

Epilogue: It Was Written in a Song

I came into the world when great love songs were still popular and honest songs of betrayal and consequence were top of the charts; Paul Simon was correct in saying there must be fifty ways to leave a lover, and it is important to know when to leave or when to tell someone to go, as suggested by Ray Charles. R.B. Greaves wrote a letter. If temptation can take you from love, the love was never honest enough to have you stay; you must know yourself and your own needs before you tell someone to hit the road and mean it. Sometimes you can love with all your heart but still need to admit defeat. Being able to see what is in front of you and having the courage to address it is an invaluable skill; moving on and learning is the hard part. In the end, maybe the adventures we have and the lessons we learn along the way are more important than the answers we utter; Pee-wee Herman may have been right in his quest to find adventure.

Right now, I have chosen to live my life surrounded by a great many loves—loves that I have confidence in. I am not married because I have learned I truly believe in love and the music it inspires. As I age, I realize I am a little picky and far too patient. But why not? It is I who will live and stand by the consequences of any *I do's* I say. I will remain picky and patient until I can answer assuredly with honesty and love, for marriage would be for the rest of my life—through thick and thin, through sickness and health.

Should the day come that I receive another proposal, again I will be facing a choice. Until then, I am just a girl who chooses to be true to herself—and who's said no five times.

Nothing more, nothing less.